COVENANT

BY: Inez R. Reilly

COPYRIGHT © AUGUST 2010 by Inez R. Reilly

PUBLISHER
SADIE BOOKS, 215 E. Camden Ave H-11 Moorestown NJ 08057 ---- 1-856-313-0548

ISBN-10: 098-1604722
ISBN-13: 978-0981604725

LIBRARY OF CONGRESS - Control Number 2010911913

BOOK LAYOUT - C ALLEN DESIGN – Interior and Exterior

OTHER PUBLISHED BOOKS BY INEZ R. REILLY
All Other Ground
How to Taste it at the End of the Day

COMING SOON
Blood Dipped
Like a Roaring Lion

PRESTON WAS LEFT BREATHLESS, as he watched Damaris walk down the aisle. He had thought of this moment, for months, and still could not have imagined a more beautiful sight.

Damaris smiled, as she witnessed the reaction on his face. Tears welled up, as she anticipated being held in his arms. She missed him. The last time she had laid eyes on Preston, was a week ago. It was a mutual agreement to allow themselves the time to commune with God, prior to their union. Now, as she caressed his face with her eyes, she was more in love than ever. She felt as if she was walking on clouds, as she moved closer and closer to the man God had chosen for her.

Preston was corralled by an intense restraint, as he stood in place waiting for his bride. A grin seemed to stretch his face, beyond its limit. He felt like he was beaming with pride. He silently thanked God (as he had done, countless times) for leading him to his destiny. Damaris Rhenay was his wife. He knew it, just as he knew his name was Preston Lambert.

I want to express my deepest
appreciation to:

Justin K. Finch

For his hard work on the cover
illustration of this book.

ACKNOWLEDGMENTS:

I give all thanks to God, Who is the Author and Finisher of my faith. He gave me the gift, to write. Therefore, He gets all of the credit.

I want to thank my children and grandson: Keilah, Joshua, Seraya, Joy and Haliek. I appreciate their encouragement and their patience, while I took time away from them to complete this project. I want to thank, my best friend Cherrie, for her prayers, words of inspiration and snacks as I sat for hours and hours working on this book. I am grateful to Cassandra Allen, my media contact at bullhorngypsy.com, who exhibits blind faith in my abilities, which encourages me to be the best that God intends. Thanks, to my Pastors: Bishop Daniel Robertson, Jr and Elena Robertson – my mentors: Pastor Katherine Corbett, Brenda Gonzalez and Brendell Francis – my "sisters:" Patricia, Anitrese, Kandice, Kenyatta, Mary, Niambi, Suzanne, Kyella, Marilyn and Mellanese – my "brothers:" Richard "Poncho", Irving, Carlos, Darryl, Anthony, Eddie, Frank and Kirk - my "girls:" Bernadette, Christina, Ronnalyn, Lori Ann, Dionte, Teshia, Margaret and Diane – the "older women:" Selma Preston and Kathleen Jones – my "other kids:" Jatajah, and Shinika – my nieces and nephews: Nicole, Michael, Lewis, Marianna, Marisol, Nick, Mo, Tony, Sylvia, Evelyn, Debra, Levone, LaToya, Nikki, Desiree, Diondre "Munch", Ashley, and Jonathan – and the countless others who have reassured and succored me through intercession – lastly, those of you who purchased this book.

Much Love,

Inez R. Reilly

iamsproperty.biz

CHAPTER ONE

Preston Lambert loved driving his car. As he sped down Interstate 64, with his briefcase and cell phone on the passenger seat, he felt abandon. This stretch of road was beautiful, at this time of year. Autumn, in Virginia, was his favorite season. He viewed the changing leaves, dangling on their branches, while the felled ones decorated the landscape with a brilliant hue and smiled. Life was good.

He recalled his day at the office. He had, finally, closed the acquisition deal he had been working on for months. His paralegal surprised him with lunch and a bottle of sparkling apple cider, to celebrate. He had given her the afternoon off. She deserved it. Ariel had been logging in the long hours, just as he had done. She created report after report, only to have several revisions cause her to start from scratch. She deserved a raise, not just an early start to her weekend.

Ariel Jackson was his first choice, when researching the pool for his paralegal. She was an intelligent go-getter, who did not require his constant attention. She had a discerning spirit, which enabled her to be tactfully proactive when dealing with him and his business. He appreciated her moxie, when approaching him with her ideas. He had learned, long ago, to trust her decisions. Preston was satisfied that he was in good hands, as far as his career was concerned. He was not afraid that she would embarrass him, when meeting with his clients. She was a top-notch professional whom he respected.

The rumor mill was circulating the news that Ariel was seeing Micah Alexander, in accounting. He was a good guy. He was hardworking and reliable. Preston believed those to be good qualities, in a man. She deserved someone who was serious about his career and knew what he wanted in life. Micah was working diligently toward his goal to become the first African-American Chief Financial Officer of Brookes & Brooks.

Preston and Micah had been close friends since their days at James Madison University. They were both, wet behind the ears, as they lugged their satchels and boxes into the dorm room. They dropped everything to introduce them selves and became instant buddies. Micah was from Long Island, New York. Preston was a native Virginian. Both Preston and Micah stood 6'3" tall. Micah's chiseled features, along with his burnt umber color, made him appear like an

Oscar award. He was lean, while in contrast Preston was muscular. Micah played basketball. Preston played football. Each man was proud to be a Duke and wore the colors well. They pledged Pi Kappa Phi, together which made them brothers.

They supported one another, without reservation. He enjoyed their double dates with a couple of the girls from the sorority Alpha Phi. He was grateful for the time he shared with his closest friend. Neither was given to strong drink, nor did they experiment with recreational drugs. Both had decided to respect their bodies, and those of the women they dated, by abstaining from sexual relationships. It was good to have a comrade, in the faith.

As graduation day approached, Preston and Micah decided they would not part company. They planned to continue to be roommates, as they embarked on their adult lives. Preston had watched Micah mature and become someone he admired, greatly. Ariel could not have chosen to accept a better man. He wished them well.

Preston roused himself from his reverie, as he approached the exit for the Chesapeake Bay Bridge Tunnel. He turned on his CD player and sang his favorite Fred Hammond song,

Keep on Praisin', from the Free to Worship CD. Although it was from 2006, he still treasured the spiritual tone of each song. This particular track was an upbeat tune that spoke about moving on when things get you down. He had come to love this selection during the days and weeks when the business of the acquisition was droning on and on. Ariel had been listening to the song on her MP3 player, during one of their late night vigils of report building. She had walked into his office to find his head in his hands and his tie on his desk. He was startled as she placed the headphones into his ears, advising he needed this more than she did, at the time. Preston had gone out to buy the CD the following day, from the local Best Buy.

Before he knew it, he was driving past Micah's home on Fallbrook Bend. He made the next right, onto Meadowside Dr. He was home. He pulled his 2009 Lexus IS 350 into place in his 3-car garage. He turned off the ignition, sat back and took a good whiff of the new car smell. He mused, again, "I love this car." He thought of the sleek design, the polished granite exterior, with its alloy rims. He smiled, as he thought of the 3.5 liter, V6 engine with its ability to go from zero to sixty in 5.6 seconds. This beauty could top speeds upwards of 143 mph. Just the thought of it gave Preston goose bumps. He deserved this delightful gift, just like the salesman had said. He felt no disappointment in his indulgence. In fact, he thought it long overdue.

Preston was startled by the persistent ring of his cell phone. He clicked the TALK button, "Hello, Preston Lambert speaking. Oh, hey Micah, what's up?"

"I am just checking to see if you wanted to take a ride out to the beach. I have something I want to run pass you." Micah sounded a bit anxious.

"I just pulled up. If you give me a bit to shower and change, I can come around in my new baby." Preston was rubbing the seats, as he spoke.

"Sure. You can just honk the horn, when you pull up. Thanks for agreeing under such short notice." Again, that note of anxiety tinged his voice.

"No need for thanks, man, you know that. I shouldn't be more than thirty minutes. You want to give me a heads up, prior to my arrival?" Preston thought he may need to prepare himself, as Micah was one given to planning ahead. It was the rare moment when he doled out spontaneous invites.

"No. I would rather wait. I think and speak more clearly on the road, you know that," Micah reminded him.

The two hung up, after their good-byes. Preston opened up the car door, as he used the remote to close the garage door. He grabbed his briefcase off of the seat and strolled into this kitchen, which was just off of the garage. He punched the code into the security system. He placed the attaché on the counter and checked for voice messages, as he took off his jacket and loosened his tie.

His mother had called to see what time he was coming by on Sunday; his sister called to remind him of the get-together at their mother's house; and one call from a random telemarketer – all of which he erased. He did not need to be reminded about visiting with his mother. He loved her, dearly, and would not miss an occasion to sit down and indulge in her good home-cooking.

Kathleen Lambert was the most honest, down-to-earth woman he knew. She did not take any junk off anyone, especially her children. She had raised them in church. She taught them the rudiment of Christian living, which they did not stray too far away from. She adored her children, and they honored her. His father, Joseph Lambert, had passed away some years ago and his mother's faith helped the family survive. They held on to God and each other, as they grieved the loss of their patriarch. His parents loved each other, very much. Their love could be witnessed by anyone who was in their company. It was this same love which blessed their home and their children. Preston hoped he would find a wife, and love her, as his father had loved his mother.

As he walked up one, of the two, staircases in his home toward the master bedroom, he thought of the time he would carry his bride up these very steps. He was filled with warm musings of his first night in this home with his wife. He thought of this often. He was ready to find his "good thing" as the Bible called her. He had followed his vision for his career and the path he had chosen was a prosperous one. He was Vice President of Litigation at Brookes & Brooks. He had worked long, hard hours and charted many billable hours for the company. He was one of the premier African American attorney's in Virginia. He was proud of his accomplishments and was ready to share his life with a good woman. He hoped to find a wife who possessed qualities like his mother.

He walked down the hall toward the shower. He entered the bedroom and removed the remainder of this clothing. He had an idea of what he would put on, after the freshening up. He did not want to have Micah waiting longer than necessary. He pulled out his Nike pants, a T-shirt, and coordinating jacket and laid them out on the bed. He moved on into the bathroom and turned on the shower. He looked forward to allowing the water to wash away any stress from the day, so he could give Micah his undivided attention.

CHAPTER TWO

Preston drove up Micah's driveway twenty-five minutes after his phone call. He blew the horn, as he had been instructed and Micah came right out. He was sporting an Adidas jogging suit, with matching sneakers. As he opened the door, he threw a bag in the backseat, and then eased into the passenger seat of the Lexus.

"Forgive me, man, for the short notice. I have had a lot on my plate, over the past couple of weeks. I did not tell you that I had, officially, applied for the Chief Financial Officer position. I had been praying and believing God for the opportunity and it had arisen. I submitted my resume, I was called for an interview and I waited." Micah turned to Preston, "I got the job, man. I am the new CFO of Brookes & Brooks."

Preston looked over at Micah and yelled out, "man, say what? You did not breathe a word of this to me! I am so proud of you. Congratulations, Micah. You deserve it. There was no one more capable or fitting for the job. Oh, my brother, you have made history in that company. You are the first African-American CFO." He reached over and patted Micah on the back, heartily. "What? Is this ride to the beach to celebrate this momentous occasion? Where would you like to go? It will be my treat."

"We, first, need to pull out of the driveway." Micah was laughing. He respected Preston's opinion and was pleased he was so enthusiastic in his accolades. He had wanted to tell him of his decision, sooner, but he had to leave it in God's hands. He chose to fast, pray, believe and wait. He was so grateful God had blessed him with the desires of his heart.

Preston shifted the gear into reverse and pulled out onto the street. He turned right onto Diamond Springs Rd and headed for Interstate 264 eastward. "You did say you wanted to ride out toward Virginia Beach, didn't you?"

"Yeah, let's get down there and find a nice quiet spot to park and walk on the boardwalk. It has been a long week and the relief of hearing of the appointment has left me with some energy. The ride will help clear away any cobwebs, and the saltwater air will do the rest." Micah settled back into the seat and sighed. This had indeed been a long week. He had been contemplating taking the next step with Ariel, but he wanted more to offer her. He knew he was on the right path, however, he desired to be securely ensconced in his career

10

before he invited her into his life, permanently. He wanted to run it past, Preston. He wanted his blessing.

Preston was lost in his own thoughts, as he accelerated onto the Norfolk/VA Beach Expressway. He recalled many nights on the JMU campus, where he and Micah walked the grounds praying about their futures. They encouraged each other, in their endeavor to remain celibate and to be men of integrity. There were many occasions when the test was pressing them, as many young ladies were not under the same restraint. It boggled their brain how persistent a woman could be when she set her mind on a matter. Yet, they held fast to their profession of faith … sometimes, with great angst. Both had endured harsh words from men and women about their choices.

As he pondered on the news of Micah's promotion, he felt like it was all worth it. Micah had put his energies on studying and advancing his mind. He used the basketball court to get out any excess aggressions. Preston was grateful, to God, it had all paid off for his comrade in the faith. The Lord was proving that He would, indeed, take care of those who put their trust in Him. He smiled and said a silent prayer of thanks for this time, in his friend's life.

He shifted lanes, on the highway, and moved past many drivers. It was a beautiful autumn evening. He felt the familiar longing to have someone of the female persuasion share these moments with. Preston knew he had a heart full of love, which he believed had been transferred to him by his father. He had been, carefully, trained to be a husband by watching his dad be one. Joseph Lambert had all the moves and Preston watched him work.

He knew, one day, he would find his bride and he needed to pay close attention to his mentor. His father never missed an opportunity to tell his mother how beautiful she was. He infrequently left the house without kissing and hugging his wife. When he arrived home, he went to her first. He exclaimed about how much he missed her and enjoyed coming home. His mother beamed under the attention and everyone was blessed because of it.

"What is that smile on your face for, man? You are over there just smiling, all the while picking up speed. You all right? You have some news to tell me?" Micah was looking over at Preston, while he spoke.

He had not realized Micah was watching him. "Naw, man, I was just thinking about my dad. I sure do miss him. Even after all of this time … can you believe it has been six years, since he passed? I have been thinking about the example he led for his children. He showed Anise, Aaron and I what a husband and father was to be. For Aaron and I how we were to be with our wives – for Anise, what to look for in a husband."

"Pop Joe was a good man, Preston. He was good to me and accepted me as one of his spiritual sons. He mentored me, as well. I am a better man because of my relationship with him. I miss him, too, man. I didn't know my father, and Pop Joe took up the call. I appreciate him for his obedience to speak into my life and change my destiny." Micah readjusted himself in the seat.

"Micah, my dad was my hero. I hope to be half the man he was when I have my family. I was thinking about how he treated my mom. She flourished, as a woman, under his attention. She never appeared nervous or anxious when in my dad's presence. He doted on her and she was a blessing to him. They did not hide their affections from us. We were taught it was okay to display our feelings to those we love. It was not vulgar or licentious, in any way." Preston felt tears fill his eyes, at the memory. He was so appreciative of God to have placed him in the Lambert family. He felt well-rounded and grounded, as a man, being raised by his father.

Preston and Micah fell silent; each wrapped up within their own cerebrations. Joseph Lambert had affected change for both of them. Preston had the opportunity to grow up surrounded by love and acceptance. Micah had been adopted into the fold, during his tenure at JMU. They matured under the hand of a mighty man of God.

Preston turned off onto Exit 20 toward Laskins Road. He had an idea of a good spot to stop, eat and have access to the boardwalk, which Micah wanted to stroll down. He made the right onto Atlantic Ave making his way toward Tortugas Café and Tiki Bar.

"I know where we are going, man. We are going to Tortugas, aren't we?" Micah was smiling. He loved this particular stretch of Virginia Beach. There were tourists, but not too many this time of year, as the season was winding down. "This should be about the last weekend, we can get into that place, before they close the grill side." He adjusted himself in the seat and looked out the window.

"Yeah, we are going to Tortugas. I figured the atmosphere would be conducive to relaxing, while you elaborate more about your musings." He slid into a parking spot, just outside the café. With the ignition turned off, he turned to Micah. "I just want to say, again, I am proud of you. Your plan is working out, because you allowed God to direct your footsteps. You have done a great job, Micah."

"Go on, man, with that mushy sentiment." He laughed, as he jokingly slapped at Preston's arm. "No, seriously, I appreciate your encouragement and constant support. I don't know how many days your allegories and inspirations were 'mot juste.'"

"Whoa, whoa, look at you pulling out the French phrases on a brother." Preston laughed goodheartedly.

"Don't embarrass me, Preston. You know what I am saying; they were the right words at the right time. God used those uplifting discussions to pull me through some rough spots, as I tarried on the road of indecision. You had no idea I had been planning on putting in my bid, at that moment. Yet, you were always there supporting me and letting me know I had the business acumen to be the head and not the tail." Micah's stomach growled, loudly. As he grabbed his belly, he said "let's take this discussion inside."

They got out of the car and walked around to the outdoor grille area. The waiter approached them and led them to a table, along the edge of the beach. He placed menus on the table and asked what would be their drink of choice. Both men ordered a non-alcoholic beer, and then settled into their seats, looking out toward the beach.

They exchanged small talk about the office and before long, "Hunter" their waiter returned with their food. They made a small feast of Buffalo wings, quesadillas, potato wedges and barbecue burgers. Hunter brought them tall glasses, of iced water, along with plenty of napkins and set them down on the table. He asked if there was anything else, they needed and took his cue when they waved him away with their hands, as their mouths were already filled with food.

Micah leaned back in the chair, "that ought to settle you down," he said aloud as he patted his stomach. Preston laughed, as he wiped the barbecue sauce off his mouth. He took a quaff of his beverage and sat back, as well.

"Now that we have calmed the savage beasts, let's get down to the business, at hand. You have something on your heart and I am all ears, my friend." Preston leaned in, so Micah would know his attention was focused on what he was about to share.

"It's about Ariel. Preston, I love her so much. I have imagined nothing else, since we have started dating, than to make her my wife. I know she feels the same and has been hoping I would pop the question, but I just did not feel quite right while I was still jockeying my way up the corporate ladder. I was thinking of her and the possible future we could have, when I decided I would put my name in the hat for CFO. Now that dream is no longer an ethereal imagining, I can focus on making her Mrs. Micah Alexander."

"Micah, you deserve to be happy, man. Ariel is a good woman. She loves you and would make you an awesome wife. It is a blessing, as you have found your treasure in an earthen vessel. Man, now that you are considering moving into the arena of marriage, there are a host of other responsibilities you must undertake. Are you ready to take the leap into headship? You have spent a great deal of time focusing on you and what your plans are for your life. Are you prepared to love Ariel, as Christ loves the church?" Preston looked, intently, toward Micah waiting for the answers. He loved him, like a brother and their relationship was such that he could ask such probing questions.

Micah shook his head and whetted his lips as he pondered his reply. "Preston, I don't know – thus the invite to take the ride and parry this thing out with you. I know I love her. I know I cannot imagine my life with any other woman. Now, how that weighs against me enjoying my space and all that entails, I cannot say, at this moment."

"Listen, we both have been bachelors for a while, now ... longer than most guys. It is going to take some time to assure ourselves that we are prepared to share our space. I don't have a special someone, just yet, so I cannot speak on that. I do know you have a great deal to offer Ariel. Your willingness to open up your heart and mind to consider marriage gives testament to your love for her. I suggest you set up an appointment with Pastor Howard to garner some wise counsel, on this subject. I think you can do it, man. However, I am not the one who has to be convinced of such, you know what I mean?" Preston searched Micah's face for a sign alerting him of his deepest thoughts on the matter.

"I walk around my house, after work, and I daydream about Ariel coming in with me. I can picture her car parked next to mine, in the garage. I have imagined us preparing dinner, together and her sitting across from me, at the table. My house seems empty since I first, told her I loved her. Sometimes, on Saturday afternoons, it seems like I can hear her in one of the rooms doing her thing. I find myself smiling thinking about watching her seated by the fireplace wrapped up in her favorite blanket. My heart feels ready to, at least, ask her to marry me. I pray I can walk it out, everyday, and she not be adversely affected by my bachelor dynasty coming to an end." Micah looked up, as Hunter approached the table.

They paid the bill, left a decent tip and meandered out toward the boardwalk. It was the perfect time to walk. The conversation was heavy with the consideration of such an endeavor. Marriage was nothing Micah or Preston took lightly. They had big shoes to fill, with Pop Joe and Mama Kat, at the forefront of their minds. Micah wasn't as sure about his ability to maintain because his father and mother were never married. He did not have early childhood memories of solid relationships and he did not want Ariel to suffer because of it. He had been reading books on relationships and his role as the head of his household. Everything he read gave room for more insecurity, yet he did not want to let Ariel get away. She deserved to have a man who could love her through good and bad times. He wanted to be that man.

Preston had been looking out toward the Atlantic Ocean, while they walked in silence. The waves were lapping the shore, ever so lightly. In the distance, he could see a Navy ship moving, slowly. The fuchsias and reds that painted the horizon were growing darker and darker, as evening gave way to nightfall. There was a bit of a chill in the air, as was not uncommon this time of year. He watched lovers walking, hand in hand, along the sandy shores. He was happy for Micah, because he would soon have the opportunity to clasp arms with his wife and promenade on the beach. Ariel was blessed, as Micah was taking the necessary steps to insure he was making the right decision before bringing her into his intimate space.

"Call Pastor Howard's secretary, Abigail, on Monday to check out his schedule. She will pencil you in, so you can take a meeting with pastor and discuss your plans. I trust him. My father went to him and instructed me to do the same, when I needed some counsel from time to time. His wisdom has been tried by the fires of many relationships. I have not heard one evil report from anyone who has had the good sense to darken his doors, at times like this."

The two, walked along the boardwalk, each lost in their own thoughts. Micah gaining the resolve to take the step, he has been dreaming about. Preston, silently, praying he would have the opportunity to ponder the same question that Micah is now considering.

They returned to the car and made the trip back home.

CHAPTER THREE

Damaris looked at herself in the mirror, one last time before turning to leave the bathroom. As she was walking through her powder room, she heard her cell phone ring in the bedroom. She hurried over to her nightstand to answer it. "Hello, this is Damaris."

"Girl, you sound so professional. What are you doing?" Ariel twisted the cord on her phone, as she sat in her chaise. "I am free and looking for something to do."

"You are, always, teasing me about my phone etiquette. I just got dressed. MJ and Sela are coming over. We just planned on scouring the neighborhood for yard sales and then attend a movie. We didn't think to ask you, assuming you would be hanging out with Micah." Damaris walked into the kitchen and looked into the refrigerator for a bottle of water. She twisted off the cap and took a sip.

"Not today. He is hanging out with a few of his college buddies from JMU. They all pledge the same fraternity and were in the same graduating class. They get together once a month, to bond." She laughed. "So, do you have room for a tag-along?

"If there was a tag-along, we would make room for her. However, you know that does not describe you. Of course, you are welcome Ariel. You did not even have to ask. The only thing that should have come out of your mouth is, 'what time should I meet you guys.' Besides, the more the merrier. We could make a day of it, like Micah and his boys. I am sure there are things we could get into and conversations we can have." She took another sip of her water, as she sat down in her favorite chair. She remembered when everyone had an opinion about her buying white leather furniture for her living room. She would not be moved. The oversized Italian leather sectional called to her. When she sat down, it seemed to envelop her in its buttery softness. She felt that same comfort as she sat down, today.

"Well then, what time is everyone meeting up? Are you meeting at your place or one of the others?" Ariel got up from her chaise and walked into the kitchen, near the telephone receiver.

"We said around nine o'clock. We don't want to get the leftovers at the yard sales. The movie starts at two fifteen. So, we figured we would take in a light brunch, and then get our grub on after the movie."

"Sounds like a plan to me. I better get a move on, if I want to look half-way decent. Love you, girl. See you in a bit."

Damaris clicked off the cell, leaned back and put her legs across the arm of the chair. She gazed out the window, silently thanking the Lord for such a beautiful day. She loved autumn. It was her favorite season. She was awed by the splendor of God's handiwork, as she appreciated the brilliant fall colors. As she looked out over the housetops, she could see the array of leaves, as they swayed gently in the wind. She sighed. "God, you are magnificent in all of Your ways," she spoke aloud.

She finished the bottle of water and relaxed. She still had about forty-five minutes before the girls would start arriving. MJ would be the first to arrive. She was always early. It would be a toss up between Ariel and Sela as to who would be next.

Damaris Rhenay and Ariel had been close friends, seemingly, since birth. She laughed to herself, at her exaggeration. Both lived in the Village Crest subdivision, in Towson Maryland. Damaris was a year ahead of Ariel, when they attended Hampton Elementary. They lived just houses apart on Stags Head Rd. The fact that Damaris' family was what many called "well-to-do" did not affect their friendship in the least. In fact, it was Ariel who taught Damaris not to pretend she was not rich. She always said, "Who cares what other people think. My mother told me that if God blesses you, there is nothing to be ashamed of. It is actually, a slap in God's face to downplay His blessings." She could still see Ariel's face and her wagging finger.

They spent much of their time together, as young girls. The two of them were inseparable. Where you saw one, you saw the other. It was as if they were meant to be sisters and not just friends, which is why it was so hard when her and her family moved from Towson to Virginia, after middle school.

As graduation day from Ridgeline Middle drew near, it was bittersweet for Damaris and Ariel. Their classmates and neighborhood friends kept asking them what they were going to do without each other. It was so frustrating trying to parry their questions because they didn't have the answers. Neither girl imagined there would come a time when they wouldn't be together. In their minds, they were never going to be apart. So, as they stood on the stage at their graduation ceremony, they cried. They were embarking on an important phase, going into high school, and they would not have the other for support. They were not consoled when their parents tried to convince them that they would get to see each other over the summer vacations. In fact, they looked aghast. 'How could they imagine that summer vacations were a fair trade-off when their lives were being ruined?'

The doorbell startled Damaris out of her reverie. She jumped up from the chair and ran to the door. "I hope you have not been ringing the bell too long, I was deep in thought." It was MJ, just as she knew it would be.

"No, I just got her. What had you wrapped up, like that?" MJ kissed her cheek and then moved past Damaris on her way to the sofa. MJ had on a pair of blue slacks, with a pink button up. Her hair was pulled back, showing off her beautiful ebony face. Her eyes, the color of onyx, seemed to dance like flames of a gentle fire. Damaris knew this was a sign that she was excited.

"What's up with that look on your face?" Damaris reclaimed her seat in the chair, across from MJ. "Your eyes are doing their happy dance." She leaned in, as if she were readying herself to hear a secret.

MJ seemed eager to share her news, but she held back. "I want to wait until Sela gets here, so I can tell you at the same time." She clasped her hands together in her lap and sat back, twiddling her thumbs.

"I understand. I imagine I would feel the same way." Damaris sat back, as well. "Ariel is coming too, by the way."

MJ looked perplexed. "What? No Micah, today? What is that all about? The, two of them have been joined at the hip, it seems; especially, these last few weeks." They both laughed.

"I know, right? I told her, it never crossed our minds to ask her if she wanted to spend the day with us for that very reason. Micah and a few of his frat brothers needed a little male bonding. Therefore, that left little ole Ariel in a quandary as to how to spend her Saturday. As a matter of fact, I was just sitting here reminiscing about our childhood, when you rang the bell."

"Tell me you were not sitting here thinking about how your parents busted up the dynamic duo?" MJ rolled her eyes, and chuckled playfully.

"They just did not realize how traumatic that experience was for the both of us. We felt like our lives had been devastated." Damaris could hardly contain her laughter. "I can laugh now, but back then it was as if my life was coming to an end."

"I cannot imagine. I did not have any close friends when I was growing up. I was a loner until I got to college and met you guys. I may never have pledge Alpha Kappa Alpha had it not been for Sela. What a time that was. It was stressful and fun, all at once. We had to memorize the code of conduct book and keep our grades up. When I think back on those times, I would not trade a moment of it." A wistful smile crossed her face at the memory.

"I know what you mean. When Ariel and I pledged Sigma Gamma Rho, it seemed like we would never get everything done and maintain our rigid course study. Some days I thought I would not make it. I thank God, Ariel was there. She was such a pillar of strength. When it appeared there would not be enough hours in the day, or fuel in the tank, she would call a 'prayer break.' She was so much stronger than I was, at that time. Her faith kept me going. We would put the books down, back away from our desks and fall on our knees. She would begin to call on the name of God, asking Him for the strength to accomplish our tasks with excellence. She prayed for renewed energies and for clarity of mind. Afterward, we would get up feeling refreshed in our bodies. I thank God for her witness. My life is a testament to her walk. I am certain she has some jewels, in her crown, because of the example she was to me." Damaris felt tears well up in her eyes. She was grateful for her sister, in the Lord. "I cannot thank God enough, for placing us on the same path."

"You need to cut it out, getting all mushy. You are going to make me cry, up in here." MJ dabbed at her eyes with a tissue she retrieved from the box on the side table. She passed one to Damaris. "It is a beautiful thing to have such a wonderful relationship. I have to tell you that I was a bit skeptical at first, watching you girls interact with each other the way you did. You just didn't see that kind of devotion, where I came from. The two of you were so loyal and committed to one another. It seemed a bit, unnatural."

"It was all we knew. It was as if God knitted our hearts, together, like David and Jonathan … I have to stop, right now. It is too much." She used the tissue to wipe away her tears. At that moment, the doorbell rang.

Both, Damaris and MJ grabbed their purses, walked toward the door and opened it. "Hey there, you guys," they chimed in unison.

"Hello there, you two." Sela was the first to speak. Her six foot frame towered over Damaris, Ariel and MJ. She leaned down to kiss the cheeks of her friends.

"Hey, Dee. Hey MJ." Ariel moved in for the customary greeting of hugs and kisses. She stood back, and looked into their faces. "It looks like you have been crying. Is everything alright?" A look of concern crossed her face, as her brow furrowed.

"We are fine, Ariel. It is Damaris' fault, talking about close friendships and how she is so appreciative. You know how mushy she can be; this time, she drug me along and had me all misty." The group laughed, as Damaris closed and locked the door.

"Whatever. You are just as mushy, if not more. She was passing out the Kleenex."

In the next moment, Sela yelled "Shotgun!" just before she dashed off of the porch.

CHAPTER FOUR

Damaris made the first left off of North Elizabeth Harbor Dr to move deeper into her subdivision. It was the annual neighborhood yard sale. She felt a bit giddy while thinking about the trinkets she would find. She has always loved yard sales. As a child, her mother used to wake her up early on Saturday mornings, to canvas the area for sales. It was their special time together. Her father would still be asleep so they would quietly ready themselves for their adventure. Her mother called it treasure hunting. She was feeling the same sense of exhilaration, as she drove down the street.

She was the only child of Franklin and Sylvia Rhenay. Her mother expressed her desire to have more children, but it just "wasn't in the cards." Damaris used to feel guilty when she saw her mom's expression grow dark, when she thought of her infertility. She blamed herself for her mother's condition. In her mind, if her birth had not been so difficult, perhaps her mother would have the other children she longed for. As she grew older, she began to resent her mother's dissatisfaction with the child she did have. She could not understand why she was not enough.

She snuck out of the house, on more than one occasion, and went to Ariel's. She would unlock the door to their utility room and Damaris would stealthily make her way to Ariel's room. They would stay up and talk. Ariel would tell her she was enough and that her mom will come around. In the meantime, she should know that she was loved by God and her. Damaris would lay her head on Ariel's lap and cry. Before they moved to Chesapeake, God had healed Damaris' heart when she accepted the Lord Jesus as her Savior.

When she thought of those times, she understood what her mother was missing. It was God. Her mother and father believed they were responsible for their own lives. They never acknowledged any higher being as being active in orchestrating the universe. Damaris and Ariel prayed for her parents, often. They still do. They believe that the Rhenay's will come to believe and accept the sacrifice Jesus made for them. Until then, she will love her parents and continue to be an effective witness for Christ.

Damaris spotted a yard, just ahead, filled with wonderful treasures. "Our first stop is to our right, ladies. Get your purses and let's begin this treasure hunt." She pulled the Nissan Altima up to the curb, with ease. They piled out, each heading in their own direction. Damaris walked over to a table of crystal figurines. She picked up several of them, giving them the "once over" just like her mom had taught her. There were minute chips, here and there, which may have gone unnoticed by a novice. She was no such beginner. She had been trained under the best.

Sylvia Rhenay would be able to spot the slightest flaw. She had a well-trained eye, gained from years and years of inspecting gemstones. Her mother would say, "See this, Damaris? Can you see the slight variation of color on this lampshade?" Damaris would not see what her mother saw, for many years. Her mind would be tempted to be drawn away by the "toy section," which consisted of some dolls spread out on a blanket. Her mother would recapture her attention, quickly reminding her that it was important to be able to discern between trash and a true treasure.

She placed the figurines back in their place and moved on. She came upon Sela contemplating the purchase of a collection of African American books. The lady was telling her they belonged to her great-grandmother, but she just did not have the room to keep them. Sela was attempting to barter with the woman and eventually haggled a few dollars off of her asking price. She was pleased with her acquisition and clasped the books in her arms like a beloved child.

"If I do not find another thing, all morning, I am satisfied. I know just the place they will occupy on the bookcase, in my living room." Her voice had the excited pitch of a child at Christmastime.

Damaris smiled, "Good find, Sela. You are the first to find her treasure. You get to foot the bill for brunch."

"What the..." Sela began to laugh as she realized Damaris was joking. "Not that it would have been a problem, mind you. I just wanted to reserve the right to choose when and how my money is spent."

"Oh yes, I understand completely." Damaris laughed and put her hand on her shoulder. "One's rights should never be usurped by another."

"Very funny, Dee." Sela rolled her eyes. "Let's head over to that table of ceramics. I have been looking for a hot chocolate set. My mom had one when we were kids and I loved wrapping my little hands around that warm mug. She had the matching carafe and everything. I was so upset, when my brother thought it was worth something and stole it. He sold it on the street for a measly sum, so he could get high. I have been searching for a similar set for myself. I have such fond memories of drinking hot chocolate while my mother told us stories. She was the best storyteller."

"I wish I had the opportunity to meet your mom, Sela. She sounds like a wonderful person." Damaris watched Sela's face to see if this moment was more than just ruminations.

"I wish all of you could have met her, Dee. She was a great role model. She never allowed the fact that she was raising five children without a father in the house. She was ridiculed for having so many kids and not being married. Yet, she never let that get her down. We all had the same father, at least; that is what she would tell us. She encouraged us to keep our heads up and never be ashamed of our family. I hated my father for leaving and causing her to work herself to death to take care of us." Sela's voice had grown gruff with anger. "And to have my brother be so ungrateful and disrespectful really gets my goat, you know, Dee? Our mother worked two jobs, so we would not go without. She kept us clothed and fed, along with a few extras."

As they drew closer to the table, they realized it was not worth the look. There were a few ceramic plates and cups, but no carafe and mug sets. They moved on to join Ariel and MJ who were discussing the validity of an authentic-looking painting. MJ seemed to be conceding, as they came within earshot. "MJ, why would the owner be parting with an original work of art? It just would make sense. They could take it to an auctioneer and get a much higher price tag." Ariel was holding up the piece and inspecting it, carefully.

"I guess you are right, Ariel. It just seems so real. The colors are faded, just so, which would cause one to take a second look. It still is a good piece of work, you have to admit." She was trying to see what Ariel was looking for.

"It is worth the money, though. You are right, it is a good piece. Are you contemplating purchasing it? It will go, perfectly, with the piece you have hanging in your office." Ariel handed the painting to MJ for further contemplation.

"You are over here looking like an auction house appraiser." Damaris walked over to look at the painting.

"Girl, you know how I do." All four laughed, causing a few hunters to look their way. "We are causing a scene, ladies, let keep it down." They laughed all the more, as they headed toward the sale proprietor to pay for the painting.

They put the items in the trunk and loaded back into the car. Damaris pulled the Altima onto the street and made a right at the STOP sign. She spotted a crowd, at the next corner. "There must be some good stuff at that house, guys. You see how many people are milling around? I hope we have not missed all of the good stuff."

"That house is mammoth, Dee. I am certain they have plenty of things to choose from. No need to worry, my friend." Ariel leaned forward and patted her on the shoulders.

"Don't joke me, Ariel. I take this very, seriously." Damaris chuckled, lightly. She circled the block, twice before she spotted a car pulling out.

When they walked up to the expansive lawn, they saw why so many people flocked to this yard. It was an estate sale. The entire house was opened up and everything had to go. Damaris nearly ran up the steps, in her excitement.

"Oh my gosh, this has got to be the best yard sale day, ever! There has to be something here, for everyone. Look at all of this stuff. There is a table full of Mikasa crystal on the left lawn. They have an entire section of antiques just inside the house." Damaris was almost squealing with glee.

Ariel and MJ walked over to the art table, behind a large oak tree. Sela hurried over to what looked like ceramics, while Damaris nearly ran inside to inspect the antiques.

When they all met back at the car, their arms were filled with their finds and their faces shone with satisfaction. Sela had found her ceramic carafe and mug set. MJ found an authentic miniature painting. Ariel was loaded down with four pair of brand new Anne Klein shoes. Damaris brought up the rear with a Faberge egg.

"What a great start to our day, huh, ladies? Everyone found what they had been

looking for and could not find anywhere else."
MJ was speaking, while she gazed out of the
window.

"Now is a good time for some brunch and
conversation. Oh yea, MJ, you said you had
some news you wanted to share with us all. Do
you want to spill the beans now, or over a nice
antipasto?" Damaris turned back, as she came
to a stop at the traffic light.

"I will make you, girls, wait just a tad
longer. Suspense is a good thing, from time to
time. Patience is a virtue and all that other good
stuff." They enjoyed another good laugh, as the
light changed and Damaris pulled out onto
Portsmouth Blvd.

"Where are we headed, Dee? Had you
guys decided where you were going?" Ariel
queried.

"We have not made a choice, so I have
taken it upon myself to surprise you ladies."
Damaris took the east ramp to Interstate 264
toward Frederick Blvd. She turned on the CD
player and the car was filled with the
instrumental sounds of Chris Botti.

Damaris pulled off the highway and took
the first left on Laskins Road. She began looking

for her destination, which came up sooner than she thought. She turned into the parking lot and found a parking space. "We are here, girls. I heard about this place from a co-worker of mine. It is a café called First Colony Coffee House."

The ladies walked into the café and were pleased with the ambience. It was just right for a Saturday brunch. As they waited to be seated, Ariel called out, "Micah."

CHAPTER FIVE

Micah thought he heard his name, just as he and the fellas were seated. The voice sounded so familiar, which is why he stood up and looked around. He was surprised to see Ariel standing in the foyer area with a small group of women. He excused himself from the table and walked over to Ariel. He was excited to see her. Here he was thinking his day was going to be spent missing her, he had the opportunity to set his eyes on his one true love.

As he was approaching, Ariel was walking toward him. His heart was pounding in his chest. He wanted to drop to one knee and propose to her, right in the middle of the café. However, he needed to restrain himself until he could meet with Pastor Howard. He, silently, prayed for Monday to arrive so he could get the ball rolling by setting up an appointment.

"Hey, baby." Micah opened his arms and welcomed Ariel with a warm hug and a brief kiss. "Fancy meeting you here." He smiled as he stepped back to look in her face. "I had no idea you knew about this place. Preston just turned us on to it, this morning." They were walking back toward the ladies.

"I had no part in this, sweetie. Damaris wanted to surprise us, so she brought us here. It was a spur of the moment thing, me hanging out with them. I was home and called Dee. She told me the girls were hanging out and I sort of invited myself." She smiled up at Micah.

"No, she did not 'just invite herself' She knows she is, always, welcome when it comes to me." Damaris chimed in, as they reached the group. "Hello, Micah. How are you doing? I have not seen you in such a long time. Ariel has been keeping you all to herself." She leaned in to kiss Micah's cheek.

"It has been a while, Damaris. How have you been?" Micah stepped back to give her the once-over. "You are looking lovely, as ever."

"Why, thank you, kind sir. I have been fine. Working more than I should be, but I love every moment of it." She smiled.

"Who are these beauties? I have not had the pleasure of meeting the two of you" Micah turned his attention to MJ and Sela. He extended his hand, "I am Micah Alexander, the love of Ariel's life." He smiled and winked to Ariel.

"Micah this is Mary Jane, we all call her MJ, and Sela. They are friends of ours, from college." She was smiling. "And yes, ladies, this is the love of my life."

MJ took Micah's, extended hand. "Hello, Micah. I am inclined to agree with you and assent that you must be the love of her life. We have had several outings of which Ariel was not in attendance, as she was spending time with you. She speaks well of you and that is a good sign." She smiled. "We are not offended that you have absconded our friend, she has never looked happier."

Sela took the proffered hand, as Micah turned to her. "Pleased to meet you, Micah. I, too, must agree with the sentiment on the floor. Any passerby would come to the same conclusion just by looking at the expression on her face, at this moment. When she realized you were here, a sunbeam burst inside of her." They all laughed.

"Well, they must see the same radiant brilliance upon my face, as well. My heart stopped, when I heard her voice; before I ever saw her beautiful face." Micah wrapped his arm around Ariel's waist. "I must confess Ariel Jackson is the love of my life, too."

"Enough of that, you guys, I am feeling a bit embarrassed." Ariel blushed, as she leaned into Micah's embrace. "Where are you guys seated? I want the girls to meet Preston." She turned to Damaris, MJ and Sela. "He is the handsome lawyer I work for. I am sure you have heard me speak of him." They all nodded.

Just then, the hostess walked up to the group, "Your table is ready, ladies. Right this way, please." She gathered a handful of menus, ready to lead them to their booth.

"We are right over there, in the corner. Get yourselves settled and join us. I will make the introductions. I must get back to them, before I never hear the end of it." Micah joked.

The hostess led Damaris, Ariel, MJ and Sela to their booth, as Micah walked back to his table. "He is cute, Ariel. No wonder you have been keeping him to yourself." Sela quipped as they placed their belongings on the seat. "He is just the right size and build for you. Have the two of you..."

"Sela! Will you stop that?" Damaris interjected. "You know good and well that Ariel has chosen to remain celibate until she is married. You should not be bringing that up causing her mind to wander." Everyone laughed.

"We all know the road to hell is paved with good intentions. We can mean to do a thing, but ..." Sela cut her eye at Ariel. "Girl, I know you know what I am talking about. It has to be hard to keep your mind from wandering without any prompting." She peered around to get a glimpse of the men at the table. "I would have to sleep with the bible on my loins and a cross in my hand, to ward off the musings of a celibate woman. I don't know how you, two, do it. Well, I know how you do it Damaris, you don't have a man." Sela laughed to show her words were in good humor.

Damaris smiled, "I must admit, without the distractions of a good man I have not been having too much trouble."

MJ had been staring at the table, as well. "I think I know one of them at the table. If I am not mistaken that is Garrison Mitchell sitting amongst them." She squinted her eyes, as if to focus. "If that is not him, he has a twin in the world. Albeit, I am certain it is."

"I hope you are right, MJ girl, cuz you are giving him a stalker's stare-down." Sela was looking at her friend's face. "What's up with that? You, two, see that dreamy look in her eyes?" Ariel and Damaris turned to look into MJ's eyes. "You see that?" Sela pointed.

MJ seemed oblivious to the attention she was getting. Her face felt flush. There was a mist of perspiration above her brow. Her heart was racing. Her mouth went dry. She didn't budge when Sela waved her hand in front of her face.

"Girls, she is in a trance. We need to snap her out of it before we walk over to the table." Sela took MJ by the shoulders and helped her sit down. "MJ, girl, what is going on with you? I have never seen you like this over some guy. Who is this Garrison Mitchell, anyway?"

The touch of Sela's hand on her shoulder caused MJ to focus on her comrades. "What?"

"MJ are you alright? You look like you have seen a ghost. You are perspiring." It was Damaris who asked the question.

"I know I must be acting oddly. I apologize. It is just that I have not seen Garrison, since our junior year in high school. He was in one of my honors science classes. We were lab partners." She turned her head and looked toward the table, again. "His mother and father were getting a divorce. He had to move away just before the Christmas break."

"Were the two of you an item? Girl, you look like he was the bomb. You all misty and stuff." Sela leaned in to hear the answer to her question.

"What? No, we were not an item." MJ answered, a bit too abruptly. "We were lab partners, that is it. He was brilliant, though. And his hands …" Her eyes wandered off, again. She could almost feel his hands touching hers, at this moment. Her mind was reeling.

Ariel and Damaris looked at each other, quizzically. "His hands?" They both chimed, in unison. Sela leaned back in the booth, her mouth opened slightly.

"Yes, he had such strong hands." MJ's voice softened as she spoke of them. "Whenever we had to do an experiment, he would grab for the switch for the burner first. Our hands would touch, because I wanted to turn on the burner, too." A whimsical look crossed her face, as she smiled. "It never failed. We would both reach for it at the same time and our hands would touch."

"Mary Jane Hall you have got to get yourself together. Micah is waiting to introduce us to his boys and I do not want you embarrassing me as you gawk over this Garrison guy." Sela looked at her friend. "Now, can we act like respectable career women and walk over to their table? Or do we have to have Ariel go over there and extend our apologies because one of us has lost our minds?"

"My goodness, Sela, I have not lost my mind. I am just surprised to see him. It has been such a long time. I worked so hard to get him out of my..." MJ paused, realizing she had put a voice to her private thoughts.

"Put him out of your what, girl?" It was Ariel. "You must have had some feelings for him, MJ. It is written all over your face. Even though so much time has passed, the sight of him is having some effect on you."

"You appear to be trembling, MJ. Are you alright?" Damaris took her hands into her own. "Your palms are moist. Girl, spill the beans. Garrison was much more than a lab partner, at least in your eyes."

MJ sighed and leaned back into the seat. "You are right. Oh my God, I did not think I would ever be saying this to another human being." She took a deep breath. "I used to fantasize about him. The thoughts would come out of nowhere, seemingly random. I would be trying to study and I would find myself writing his name on my paper. I would be asleep and the most sinful visions would dance in my head. I would awake to sweat-soaked pajamas. Girls, he was perfect, in my eyes. And when I saw him over there, all of the feelings I had been pushing to the back of my mind came flooding to the surface. I could not catch my breath for a moment. He was the most exquisite man I had ever imagined, at least in my eyes. No one has ever measured up to the standard he set in my psyche."

"You loved him, MJ. I hear the passion in your voice. It's the same passion I feel when I am talking about Micah. Oh my goodness, even after all this time, it is still there." Ariel was smiling at MJ.

"Does he know? Did you ever tell him how you felt, MJ?" Damaris was smiling, as well. It all sounded so romantic. MJ was facing her long lost love.

"Ladies, let us not keep her in this state. We still have to go over to the table. Now back to my question. Will you be able to walk over there, with your head held high, like a respectable lady? There is nothing worse than seeing a woman fawning over a guy. I never expected this from you, MJ." Sela looked appalled.

"Don't be mean, Sela. Just because you have a 'thing' against men, does not mean we all have to have one. Some of us do want a man for more than just what is in his pants." Damaris rolled her eyes and swatted Sela on the arm.

"Whatever. No matter what you say, what is in the pants does matter. Don't fool yourself, okay? It matters, a lot. You will find out, baby girl." Sela laughed. "MJ, are you in control of yourself?"

"Sela, I am fine. I will not embarrass you, alright?" MJ rose from the seat and dabbed a napkin on her face.

"You look fine, MJ." Damaris assured her.

"You sure?" MJ questioned.

"I am positive." Damaris smiled.

"Can we get this taken care of, already? I am hungry." Sela exclaimed, as she began to move toward the corner table, as directed by Micah.

CHAPTER SIX

Micah returned to the table and took his seat. The waitress had come around to take their order for drinks. Preston had ordered him large Coke, with lemon, which was his standard. The guys were laughing, as he sat down.

"We saw you over there talking to that group of ladies. Does Ariel know you are such a flirt?" Garrison exclaimed. "We could not get a good look at them, I hope they are worth the trouble you will be in, when she finds out." They all laughed.

Garrison Mitchell was sitting comfortably in his seat, with is legs crossed. It was not often he would find a restaurant with tables high enough to accommodate his long frame. He was sporting a camel colored leather blazer, with a chocolate brown shirt and matching pants. He sported a pair of size fourteen shoes, which complimented the outfit, nicely. He was what the clothing industry considered "big and tall." He stood six feet five inches and weighed two hundred fifty pounds of solid muscle. He enjoyed working out, with weights, and it showed. He commanded attention wherever he went. With all of the attention, he was a humble man. His mother would have it no other way.

"I will have you know that Ariel knows just about everything there is to know about me, my friend." Micah shot back. "Anyway, it was Ariel and her friends. Damaris surprised them with this place, just like Preston did with us. I thought I heard Ariel call my name, that is why I walked over in the first place."

"You heard her call your name? Dude, we did not hear your name. How could you have, amidst all of the conversations going on in this place?" Jeremiah inquired. He leaned back in his seat and stretched his long legs out into the aisle.

Jeremiah Marquette seemed in stark contrast to Garrison. He was lean, almost skinny. He was tall and lanky, but not nearly as tall as Garrison. He felt confident in his six foot, one hundred sixty pound body. He was not offended when people would remark about his weight. He understood everyone had his or her lot in life, and Jeremiah had come to terms with his, a long time ago. He did not try to hide himself behind baggy clothes, as some other guys. He wore his pants, fitting, as well as his shirts. He had on a pair of navy blue pants, white shirt and navy blue Timberlands, today.

"Yes, I heard her call my name. I would know her voice, anywhere. It is distinctive, only to my heart." Micah said. "Preston, you understand, don't you?"

"I do, indeed. I expect when I find my one and only I will be able to hear her voice just as distinctly." Preston had Micah's back, in this. He was happy his friend had found love. He was, also, glad it was with a wonderful woman.

"Hello, gentlemen." Ariel interjected as they walked up to the table. "Hey Preston. Imagine my surprise when I saw you sitting over here. My friend, Damaris, found this place and thought it would be cool for us to eat here, before we tackled the rest of our day."

Micah stood, first, and the rest of the gentlemen followed suit. Micah spoke, "I hope I get everyone's name, correct. We have Mary Jane, MJ for short. Then there is Sela, Damaris and my sweetie, Ariel." Each woman nodded, as her name was mentioned. Each man extended his hand, as they were introduced. "On this side of the table, we have Garrison, Jeremiah and Preston."

As Garrison took MJ's hand, he held it longer than the others. He gazed, intently, into her eyes. "Mary Jane Hall, is that you?" A wide grin spread across his face. "Well, I'll be d..." He stopped himself. "Please forgive me. It has been a long time since I have been in the company of … MJ? Is that what they are calling you, now?" He stepped out from behind the table and pulled MJ into an embrace. When he stepped back, he looked down at her upturned face. The intensity in their gaze was palpable to the others. So much so that no one was surprised when he took her face into his hands, leaned down and kissed her. It was a slow, knowing kiss of longtime lovers. MJ's arms reached around his back.

"Well, I guess these two already know each other." Micah and the others laughed.

Garrison and MJ broke the embrace, embarrassed. "Garrison Mitchell. It has indeed been a long time." Her voice sounded breathy and deep. Her eyes were smoldering and her body trembled slightly from the kiss. She would never have dreamed Garrison would have reacted in such a manner. They stood there, for a long moment, before they turned to the others.

Garrison cleared his throat. "We went to high school together. We had a couple of classes in common and were lab partners."

"Looks like you were more than just lab partners, the way you enveloped her face with your mouth." Sela was not one for mincing her words. Damaris, Ariel and MJ glowered at her.

"Forgive me, again. I don't know what came over me. We were not even in a relationship, when we were in school. Although, I had secretly wanted nothing more than to date her." Garrison replied.

"What?" MJ was feeling hijacked by her emotions. She could not control the trembling and it was heard, in her voice. "Garrison, I never knew."

The patrons, at the surrounding tables, began to look over them. Micah waved for a waitress to see if they could get a larger table to accommodate everyone.

"Why don't you ladies gather your things and join us. I do not know why I did not suggest that, in the first place." Micah stated, as the waitress approached.

"That is a great idea." Garrison said.

"Yes, I believe it is." Preston said, as he smiled toward Garrison and MJ. He had never seen Garrison be so spontaneous, yet it seemed so right. Preston stepped out from his chair and offered to assist the ladies with their belongings. They assured him they would be fine, as they walked away.

"Yo, what was that all about Garrison? I have never seen you so enamored with a woman, before." Jeremiah spoke up. "It was like you could not control yourself. You, of all people; Mr. Control, himself."

"I don't know what it was. When we had to move while I was in the eleventh grade, I was mortified. Not so much because I had to go to a new school, so close to graduating, but because I would be leaving Mary Jane. I never voiced how I felt, because I thought she wasn't interested. She was all about the books, especially in our science classes. I used to find reasons to touch her hands. They were, always, so soft. In lab, I would reach to light the Bunsen burner, just as she would reach for it. She seemed like the perfect match for me. She was beautiful and intelligent, a hard combination to come by, you know?" All of the men nodded, in agreement.

The waitress found a table and everyone walked over. The men held out the chairs for the women to sit, and then took their seats. The waitress brought over the men's drinks and the women ordered their own. No one noticed that

Garrison had taken hold of MJ's hand, under the table.

"So, Mary Jane … or would you prefer me to call you MJ?" Garrison asked.

"MJ will be just fine, Garrison." She smiled, enjoying the warmth of his hands on her own.

"Well MJ, what have you been up to? What have you been doing with yourself?" Garrison looked, intently into her eyes. It was as if no one was around.

"After high school I went to Morgan State University. That is where I met Sela, Ariel and Damaris. I have a Science of Nutrition degree and I am a nutritionist at the Dominion Counseling and Wellness Center."

"Excuse me. I don't mean to interrupt." Preston leaned closer. "Did I hear you say you work at the Dominion Counseling and Wellness Center?"

MJ turned to Preston. "Yes. Have you heard of it?"

"My brother's girlfriend is the head therapist and Director of the Center. Tamu Singletary is her name."

"Yes. What a small world. Tamu is a sweetheart." MJ smiled, her response.

"She is, indeed. They have been dating for quite a while. We are all wondering why they have not tied the knot." Preston added.

"Aaron Lambert is your brother? I can see it now. He comes by, from time to time. What a character!" MJ laughed.

"He is that. Well, I will have to tell Tamu that I met you. Again, excuse me for the interruption." Preston turned his attention to the rest of the table, while Garrison and MJ got caught up.

"Well, Jeremiah, I am the Director of Information Systems…" Damaris was saying as he returned to the general conversation at the table. "I love what I do, which makes it very rewarding. What about yourself?"

Jeremiah never missed a chance to talk about himself. "I have my own accounting firm. It was math that caused my path to cross Micah's. I met Preston, as a result of becoming buddies with him. I, too, enjoy my work." He sipped on his beer and sat back.

"Nothing wrong with loving your work. There are so few people who enjoy their jobs.

We seem to be one of the lucky ones, Jeremiah." Damaris turned, in her chair, to face Preston. Her knee brushed against his leg, in the process. "Excuse me." She said, a little surprised. She did not expect his legs to be this close. "What about you, Preston? Do you enjoy the career path you have chosen?" She smiled.

"As a matter of fact, I do. I believe God called me to the legal field and He allowed me to choose corporate law. Since, I followed His lead, I have been successful. He has caused me to find favor and be promoted to Vice President of Litigation." He repositioned his legs, under the table, after the brief touch. "I am a blessed man, if you do not mind me saying so."

"I do not mind, at all." Damaris was pleased to hear a man speak of the Lord, in such a manner. "It is quite refreshing to be in the company of a man who does not boast of accomplishing all on his own. We are, all, who we are because of God. I believe that."

Jeremiah turned his attention to Sela, who had been perusing her menu. "So, Sela, what gives with you?"

"Right now, I am hungry and wish this waitress would come on over here to take our order." Sela remarked, as she sat the menu down and looked around for the waitress.

Micah chimed in. "I am hungry, myself, Sela. Where is that waitress?"

The food arrived, the drinks were refilled and the conversation never ceased. After another refill, the ladies excused themselves to the restroom and the fellas took care of the tab.

"Oh my goodness, MJ. How did you manage to stand up to that kiss Garrison planted on you? It seemed so intense and very personal." Ariel spoke from the stall. "I am not sure how I could have, if Micah kissed me like that."

"Wait a minute. What do you mean, if Micah kissed you like that? You guys have not shared a passionate kiss?" Sela was flabbergasted.

"We are not talking about me, Sela. This is about MJ and Samson." Ariel and Damaris laughed, at the comparison.

"To tell you the truth, I do not know. I was taken aback by the kiss. It was the most sensual experience I have ever had. I could not have dreamed of a more romantic reunion with the man of my dreams." MJ was at the sink,

60

washing her hands, as the others joined her. "I am going to give him my number, so we will never lose touch, again. I am assuming he is single with the way he kissed me, so I do not have to worry about stepping out of bounds."

"Even if he was seeing someone, that would have nothing to do with you. Apparently, he is feeling you. And you know how the saying goes, 'All is fair in love' she would be S.O.L." Sela retorted.

"Not in my book." MJ replied.

"I am glad to hear you say that, girl." Damaris said. "It would be horrible to encroach on another woman's territory. If he were seeing someone, you would not want to be bothered with Mr. Man. It would make it like so many of the other men, out there."

"Humpf. To each his own, is how I feel." Sela dried her hands and headed toward the door. "I just hope they paid the bill." MJ, Ariel and Damaris shook their heads and moved to leave the restroom.

When they arrived back to the table, and found the bill had been settled, they looked at each other. Sela had this look on her face, which caused them to smile to themselves.

"What is amusing you, ladies?" Micah asked, as he helped Ariel on with her jacket.

"Nothing, you fellas would be interested in hearing, believe me." Sela replied for everyone.

Garrison walked over to MJ to assist her with her things. "I would like to see you, again, if that is possible. Unless you are otherwise attached. I know it is a little late to ask that question … are you?"

"What? 'Otherwise attached?' I am not, Garrison. I would love it if we could keep in touch. Here is my card." MJ reached into her purse and handed the high gloss, embossed business card to him. Garrison, in turn, reached inside his jacket and pulled out his card. "My cell phone number is listed on the card. How about yours?"

"My number is on the card, as well. When you are in sales, you want to be reachable. One never knows when the big account will come in, you know what I mean?" Garrison smiled. "I will be calling you, next week. Is that alright?"

"That will be fine, Garrison." It was MJ's turn to surprise him. She reached up, put her arms around his neck and very softly brushed her lips against his. In the same moment, she whispered, "I will be waiting."

"Nice to meet you, Preston." Damaris said. "I have been refreshed by the conversation of a man who appears to love the Lord. I hope to see you, again."

"I would like that. I must admit, I enjoyed your company. It is good to see a woman of means who takes her relationship with God, seriously. Or so it appears." Preston raised his eyebrow, in question.

"Indeed, I do, Mr. Lambert. Indeed, I do." She turned to her friends. "Well, ladies, we must be off. The movie starts in forty minutes."

They walked out together; each group got into their respective vehicles and drove off.

CHAPTER SEVEN

Kathleen Lambert stood in her kitchen, engulfed in her own thoughts. Oftentimes, she would get caught up, thinking about Joseph. They had been married for forty years, before the Lord called him home. She missed him, every day. He was her first love, in every aspect. She knew she should be letting go. It has been six years, since his death. Yet, the memories kept her hostage, it seemed. She did not want to let her children know that she was still grieving the loss of her late husband. They have enough to deal with; losing their father has its own hardships. She did not want to have them worry that she was not able to move on. She must make a mental note to speak with Mama Salester, Joseph's mother.

She shook herself free, of her reverie, just in time to see Preston pull his car into the driveway. He was coming over for Sunday dinner. He was always, the first of the children to arrive. She wiped her hands on her apron as she walked to open the door.

"Hello, baby." Kathleen said, as she placed her arms around Preston's neck. "How have you been, today?"

Preston returned the hug, "My day has just gotten better." He smiled and kissed his mother's cheek. Kathleen beamed up, at her son, as they walked back into the kitchen hand in hand.

"Tell me all about your week, Mama." Preston stated, as he took his customary seat in the breakfast nook. He turned his gaze to his mother, so she would know she had his undivided attention. "I know you have some story to tell about some kid or professor at the University." He smiled.

Kathleen had been a professor at Norfolk State University, since her children were school age. She enjoyed teaching freshman English, as it gave her opportunity to delve into the imaginations of youth. She believed the job kept her young, at heart ... along with her grandson, David, of course.

"Believe it or not, Preston, those children acted like they had a bit of sense," she laughed. "There wasn't much shenanigans going on, at all. The professors must take their cue from the students, because they were well behaved, as well." They both laughed, as Kathleen put a piece of sweet potato pie in front of her son.

"You sure do know me, Mama. I was thinking about your sweet potato pie on the ride over here. You make the best pie. Don't tell Grandmother I told you that or I will be forced to deny it." He chuckled as he shoveled a forkful of pie into his mouth. He sat back and closed his eyes. "Just like I like it. I can taste the pudding in the mix."

"Ssshh, don't let my secret out of the bag." Kathleen laughed, as she returned to the stove to check on the fried chicken breasts, macaroni and cheese and collard greens, which were close to being finished.

"Don't you worry about that, Mama. Your secret is safe with me…that is, until I marry. I will, then, ask your permission to divulge your information." Preston sat back, after he finished off the pie.

"Married, huh? I am looking forward to the blessing that you will bring into this family. Your father will be smiling down, from heaven, on that day. I am sure of it." Kathleen's eyes glazed over, slightly.

"Mama, I miss him, too. It is hard to believe it has been six years. It seems like it was just yesterday, I was sitting in this very seat listening to his wisdom. He has influenced my life and the lives of a lot of my friends. He was a great man." Preston rose from the table, walked over to his mother and pulled her into his arms. Her tears flowed freely, as she laid her head upon his chest.

"It shouldn't still be this difficult to speak about him, baby." She removed a tissue from the pocket of her apron to dab her eyes.

"Mama, you and Pop spent forty years together. You raised a family and stockpiled wonderful memories. It is understandable for you to miss him. You spent more years together, than apart." He looked down at his mother, with concern. "Have you spoken to someone about it, Mama?"

Kathleen stepped away and wiped at her eyes. "I was just thinking I may talk with Mother Salester. She is wise and I trust her. What do you think, Preston? I did not want to bother, you kids, about it ... but it is not getting any better."

"Mama, do what you need to get some closure. Anise, Aaron and I have each other, so we can discuss our feelings of losing Pop. You need an outlet for yourself with someone who understands what it is like to lose a spouse."

"Enough of this, son. Your sister and brother will be here any minute, now. I do not want them to see me this way. I did not want you to see me this way, for that matter." She placed a wry smile on her face and went back to the stove. "I will make a point of speaking with Mother Salester, this evening, after everyone has gone. She will be staying with me a couple of days, while her house is being painted."

"When will she be coming over? Usually, she is here when I get here." Preston asked, as he took his seat.

"She decided she wanted to stay back at church for the Silver Years meeting. She has made several friends, since the group has started. It was a good idea to open the cell up to non-members, in the neighborhood." Kathleen turned off the stove and the oven. "Everything is complete. We can take this party into the living room and wait for the others." She took off her apron and draped it on the knob on the pantry door.

As she did so, Preston could remember the countless times he had watched his mother hang her apron on that knob. The kitchen had been updated, just before his father died, yet he still thought he could see the floral wallpaper that used to hang on the walls. He recalled wondering why they did not just have regular paint, like the other homes on the block.

He smiled, to himself, at the silly revelry of youth. He wanted to have such memories with his family. He wanted to build a life, for his children, as his parents had done for him and his siblings. He wanted to watch his wife develop habits that their children would one day think back on and smile, just as he was doing right now.

There were many memories of family game night, at the kitchen table. There were many late night talks, with his father, where he gleaned wisdom. He reminisced about the arm wrestling matches he had with Aaron, as he tried to prove he was stronger than his older brother. He, also, remembered his father secretly advising he should let him win a couple, to boost up his confidence. Then the one day, Aaron had won, all on his own and admitted he knew Preston was letting him win.

"You coming, Preston?" Kathleen had broken through his daydream, as he had not yet joined her in the living room.

"Yes, Mama." He smiled, to himself and walked out of the kitchen.

Preston's mother patted the seat, next to her, inviting him to join her. He walked over and sat down. "Let's turn on the game, son. Who is playing, this week?"

"Baltimore and Pittsburgh are playing on Fox and Buffalo is playing New Orleans on CBS." Preston picked up the remote. "Which will it be?"

"Let's watch the Ravens beat up on the Steelers." She smiled, as he switched the channel.

"Or the Steelers serve up a loss to those Ravens." He laughed. His mother seemed to never be rooting for the same team, as Preston. He enjoyed the playful rivalry they entertained, on Sundays during football season.

"We'll see about that, sonny boy." Kathleen chuckled. "I believe my Ravens are undefeated, so far, this season. I seem to recall the Steelers taking an "L" last week, against Tampa Bay." She continued to jibe.

"One loss does not determine an entire season, mother dear. I think someone will be eating crow, when this game is over." They both laughed.

70

Mother and son nestled into the couch, each cheering for their respective teams.

CHAPTER EIGHT

Anise Nobel held her son's hand, as they made the trek up the walkway, headed toward her mother's door. She wore a simple orange sundress, with matching sandals. Her camel-colored Coach purse, hung loosely from her shoulder. Her hair fell just passed her shoulders, in an upsweep flip-style. Her amber skin was aglow, in the afternoon sun.

Desmond, her husband, was not far behind carrying the baby bag and shopping bags filled with soda. He was of average height and build. He had a beard and mustache, which he kept cut close to his face.

"David, sweetie, be careful climbing the stairs." Anise offered, as her eighteen month old often attempted to navigate the steps, on his own. David Noah Nobels was a bow-legged little tyke. His skin tone resembled his father's, which is akin to the color of a walnut's shell. His hair was kept close to his scalp, as he was not fond of getting his hair combed.

Just as he ambled up to the first steps, Preston opened the door and swooped him up into his arms. "Hey there, big fella! How is my favorite nephew?" David squealed, with glee, as he was tossed up into the air, several times.

Preston, then hugged him close and put him down, safely, on the top of the stairs. "Hello sis. Hello Desmond." He wrapped his arms around his sister and kissed her cheek. "Do you need any help with those bags, brother in law?"

"If you don't mind, would you take the shopping bag?" Desmond reached out his hand, with the bag and Preston took it from him and they all walked into the door.

Kathleen had her grandson, on her knees, showering him with kisses. "Grandma loves her baby!"

"I love my grandma!" David giggled, in response.

"Hello, mama." Anise said, as she hugged and kissed her mother. "I'm sure glad to be here. I have missed you, this week. I feel like we haven't had any time to ourselves. We need to make time to do lunch and go to the spa. Would you like that?" She questioned.

"Of course, I would love it!" Kathleen exclaimed. "Let us plan a mother-daughter day, this weekend." She looked at her daughter. "Is that too soon?"

"Are you kidding? I wish it could be tomorrow." The two of them shared a laugh.

"It is, always, good to see you, Desmond. How are you feeling?" Kathleen hugged her son-in-law and kissed his cheek.

"I am doing great, Ms. Kathleen. Running after David is keeping me on my toes. I do not know how people do it with more than one." Desmond stated, as he put David's bag down, next to the couch in the living room.

"The adjustment is made, somehow. I don't know how Joseph did it with Preston and the twins. He never made them feel less important than the other." Kathleen stated, as she walked back into the kitchen, behind David.

"He must have had a gift." They all laughed as they made their way into the kitchen, as well.

"He was gifted, in many areas." Preston stated.

"Yes, he was. I still miss him, at times." Anise chimed in.

"We all do. Pop was a tangible force, in the lives of many. It is hard not to miss him." Preston stated, as he looked over to his mother. He grabbed her hand. "God will give us the grace to keep it moving, in the right direction, as it pertains to how we deal with our loss."

The doorbell rang, just before the front door opened. Salester Lambert ambled into the foyer, and then closed the door behind her. "Hello, family."

Kathleen, along with the others, rushed into the living room to greet the matriarch of the family. Salester was a feisty eighty-five year-old, with a beautiful crown of silver hair. She was a tall woman, with a full figure. She commanded attention, whenever she walked into a room. It had not, only to do with her size, her presence was alluring. She was a lovely woman and it was not just her outward appearance. Her spirit was calm and peaceful. Her skin seemed to exude an aura of godliness that caused people to want to be in her presence.

"Hiya, great grandmother!" David yelled, as he grabbed her legs and gave her a squeeze.

"Whoa baby boy, be careful, before you knock me down." Salester laughed, as she leaned down to pat her great grandson on the head. "I am glad to see you, too, sweetie. Let's go sit down on the couch and love on each other." David took her hand and they walked, together into the living room. There, she greeted the rest of her awaiting family, as she sat down with David.

"How did you enjoy the meeting, Mother?" Kathleen asked.

"The meeting was lovely. I had a chance to see all my friends and get reacquainted. We laughed and talked about the goodness of the Lord, and glad we are still in the land of the living to enjoy it." She laughed. "Preston, baby, would you mind taking my bag up to my room? It is right there in the foyer, next to the staircase." She pointed in the direction of her bag.

"Of course, I do not mind, Grandmother." He leaned down and kissed her cheek, just before doing her bidding.

"Thank you, baby." She replied. "Oh, I see the football game is on. Kathleen, are the Ravens doing what they need to, so we can end the week with a win?"

"Mother, I believe Preston has jinxed us, this week; they are playing horribly, so far." Kathleen stated.

"I do not see why you all love football. It seems so monotonous, to me." Anise stated, as she bent down to kiss her grandmother. "I never understood the hype, even when I was a kid. I wanted to get involved because everyone, else, seemed so excited." She laughed. "However, I have learned to be in the midst, without loving the activity. Family time is still family time."

"You are right, sweet angel. We should, always, make the most of family time. We never know when the Great Trumpet will sound, so we need to enjoy one another while we still can." Salester said, with her eyes glued to the television set.

Desmond sat next to Salester, on the sofa, and took David off of her lap. "Give Great Grandmother's lap a break, lil man. Come sit on my lap and let's watch television, until it's time to wash up and eat."

Kathleen and Anise walked back into the kitchen to get the dishes out for the meal. They set the dining room table, as was their custom. Their conversation was hushed, so as to not disturb the others watching the game.

"Kathleen, where is Aaron? He is not, usually, this late for dinner." Salester called from the living room.

"He had to ride out to Portsmith to pick up Tamu. Her car is in the shop, being serviced.

The two of them should be here, shortly." Kathleen called back, from the dining room.

"Oh, ok. I was just being nosey." She laughed.

"I don't know if I would call it that, but feel free to speak of it, as you wish."

The front door opened, shortly, afterward. "Hello, everyone." It was Aaron. He was carrying a grocery bag. "Hey Mama, I brought some ice cream, in hopes that there is a pie or some cake in the fridge."

"Isn't it just like you to be considerate enough to bring the toppings for your expectation of dessert?" Kathleen said. She reached up to wrap her arms around Aaron's neck and kiss his cheek. "How is my handsome son?"

Aaron Lambert stood six feet five inches, with broad shoulders and long limbs. His cheekbones were pronounced and were covered with a tapered beard. He wore a tailored linen suit, made from the same clothier that Preston used, as their builds were similar. He kept his hands and his feet, manicured. He wore stylish glasses, which complimented his features quite well.

"I am doing great, Ma. How about you?" He smiled down, at his mother.

"I am good, now that my entire family is here. Tamu, I am glad you could join us, today. It is always a pleasure to have you." Kathleen kissed her cheek and the three of them walked into the living room, with the others.

"I wouldn't miss a meal, at your table, if I can help it." Tamu said.

Tamu Singletary and Aaron had been, dating for over four years, now. When they met, she had just returned to the States from Europe. She had been visiting some of the universities, over there, lecturing on Psychology. She owned her own private practice, in Portsmouth, Dominion Counseling and Wellness Center. She was three years his senior which caused her pause, in the beginning. However, when she looked at the dashing, tall and good looking man, she could not resist the connection. He had asked for her number, she gave him her card and he did not hesitate to send roses to the Center the very next day. Thus, his wooing began and he has not let up, since.

"Well, now that everyone is here, we can make our way to the dining room for our meal." Kathleen stated.

"Hello, Mother Lambert." Tamu greeted.

"How are you doing, baby?" Salester returned.

"I am doing well. Thank you, for asking."

The men pulled the chairs out for the women and waited until they were seated before taking their seats. Preston sat at the head of the table, where he bowed his head and blessed the food, as well as the fellowship.

CHAPTER NINE

The last of the food and dishes had been put away. The children and grandchildren had said their goodbyes and retreated to their separate abodes. Salester and Kathleen sat in the kitchen, sipping on chamomile tea. The two women sat, in silence, for a few moments before Salester spoke.

"I noticed a sadness behind your eyes and in your spirit, Kathleen, today. Is there something you would like to talk about, sweetie?" Salester touched her hand with her own.

Kathleen put her teacup on the saucer and turned to her mother-in-law, with tears in her eyes. "I do need to talk to you, Mother."

Salester moved her chair closer to Kathleen's so she could wrap her arms around her daughter-in-law. Neither said a word, as the tears ran down her cheeks, unchecked.

"Tell me."

"I cannot ..." Kathleen begun, with a fresh batch of tears cascading down her face. "I do not know..." Her eyes were pleading with Salester to help her. "How did you do it,

Mother? How did you manage with the ache and the emptiness when your husband died?"

Salester took her time, before she answered. "Baby girl, it doesn't go away. I had to ask the good Lord to help me to live without him. I mean, truly, live. Of course, I was still alive, but something dimmed, when Arthur died. I had centered, so much, of myself around that man that I had no clue how do function without him. I do not know how long it took for me to stop looking and listening for him, in the house."

"Sometimes, I do not want to go on, without him, Mother. I know that sounds, awful, but it is true. My body still yearns for him ... I hope that is not too much information, but I need to tell it to someone." Kathleen said.

"I'm a woman, too, now." Salester laughed. "I know what it is to long for a man. So, do not be ashamed. I have often wondered how you continue to sleep in the bed you shared, with my son. I had to leave my marriage bed, when Arthur passed on. It was too painful."

"I stay in the bed, hoping he would come back to me. How crazy is that? I lay there, at night, almost willing him to come to me, just one more time. Am I insane?" Kathleen looked questioningly at her mother-in-law.

"Sugah, we all grieve, differently. I left the bed, because I could not imagine laying there and not feeling him close."

"I stay because I do not want to imagine laying there and not feeling him. I have spent too many nights, crying. I pray for God to let Joseph return to me. I know, in my head, that he is dead and will not return. I know in my head that what I am feeling needs to be put in check or it can get out of hand. I do not want to give room to the enemy to have me go over into delusional thinking. However, my heart will not let him go." Kathleen cried afresh.

"Kathleen, grieving is not an easy process. It becomes harder, still, when we refuse to allow the light of day to shine in our darkness. You are doing the right thing, by bringing this to the light, sweetie. Do not hide the torment...expose it, and be made free. I am glad you trust me to lay down your burden. There will be no room left for the enemy to come against your mind. We need to pray and beseech the Father, in heaven, to deliver you from the tormentor." Salester took both of Kathleen's hands, in her own. "You ready, baby? I know you may not feel ready, in your heart to let him go … but, do you realize the necessity of getting free from the ties that are binding you to the past?"

Kathleen nodded her head, as the sobs wracked her body. She wailed from deep within her soul, as Salester called on the name of the Lord, on her behalf.

"O God, only You know what Your daughter needs. She needs You to deliver her from the snare of the enemy. You said blessed are those who mourn, because they will be comforted. Lord, You are a great big God and You do not lie to Your children. Comfort Kathleen, O God. Touch her, deep down in her spirit. Wrench the hand of the devil from this child's heart, right now, Father. I declare and decree that she be made free from this torment. O Holy One of Israel, stay the rushing waters and quiet the raging seas; cause the storm to cease and the winds to be still, in the name of Jesus. She is free, because she has shined the light of truth on her situation. Nothing remains hidden, therefore, she cannot be held captive, any longer. O God, O God, O God, help her! Be a right now Help in her times of trouble. Dry her eyes. Be the Balm in Gilead and apply the salve to her wounded and aching soul, right now, Jesus. We will be careful to give Your name the praise...all glory and honor belong to You. We expect signs to follow our belief, in this...Amen!"

Salester stood and helped Kathleen to her feet. She held her in her arms until her body stopped shaking and the tears slowed.

CHAPTER TEN

Preston sat in his office, looking out of the panoramic window behind his desk. His mind was not on his work, today. It had been two weeks, since he had met Damaris Rhenay, and he has not been able to get her off of his mind. She was beautiful, seemed to have a good head on her shoulders and she spoke of the Lord, as if she had a relationship with Him. He did not want to overstep God, in choosing his wife, yet he could not shake the feeling that he wanted to get to know her better. He could just kick himself for not asking her for her number, the day they met. He thought of asking Ariel, but that seems so juvenile. Yet, the vision of her haunts his every waking moment. She has even invaded his dreams. He felt his face grow flush as he remembered a very vivid dream he had just had, a few days ago. He was amazed at where the mind can go, even when it is not evoked or engaged.

He was startled by the sound of the intercom, as Ariel called in to him. "Preston, you have a call on line three. It is Garrison Mitchell. Shall I put him through?"

Preston smiled. Ariel sure did have a way with words. "Yes, you shall."

"Stop teasing me, Preston." Ariel said, as she put the call through.

"What's up man?" Preston asked, in greeting.

"I just called to talk to you about MJ. Do you remember her? She was at the restaurant, a couple of weeks ago." Garrison recanted.

"Sure, I remember. What about her?"

"Well, you know we knew each other in high school and how I told you I had a crush on her, back then?"

"Uh huh."

"Well, we connected over the weekend. I just had to talk to someone about her. She is amazing, man. Her intellect is out of this world. What a refreshing moment to be able to speak, freely and not have to dumb down my conversations. I do not have to be ashamed to be an intelligent black man. We had such a good time. We wanted to keep the atmosphere free from expectations, so we went to the Olive Garden. We shared a bottle of Merlot, while enjoying each other's company." Garrison rushed on. "I'm thinking about going exclusive, man."

"Whoa, whoa-wait a moment. You mean to tell me MJ has gotten to you like that? You willing to give up your player card?" Preston laughed, but he knew Garrison was serious.

"Preston, it seems that all the feelings I had locked away, since high school, came flooding back. I have imagined myself holding my breath until I saw her that day. Does that make sense? Man, please let me know that I am not going crazy or moving too fast."

Preston thought of Damaris and how she has captured his mind. "A man knows when he has found the one. He is more certain, sometimes, than females when they think they have found Mr. Right. I will ask you this, have you prayed about it?"

"I have done nothing but prayed, since I saw her when we were together, last. I have sat, in silence, and waited for God to speak to me about her." Garrison confessed.

"What did you hear?"

"Good thing." Garrison stated, simply.

"What?"

"That is what I heard."

"Dude, you heard those words, exactly?" Preston could not contain the excitement in his voice. Garrison was not his most spiritual friend, however, he was an honest man.

"Yes, that is why I am calling you. Is that my sign, man? Is that the Lord?"

"Garrison, that sounds like God was telling you something. There is a scripture, in the bible ... hold on, let me get it, so I can read it exactly how it is written." Preston turned back to his desk and opened his top drawer to pull out his bible. He flipped through the pages, until he came to the familiar passage; "It is in the book of Proverbs, the eighteenth chapter and the twenty-second verse, Whoso findeth a wife findeth a good thing, and obtaineth favor of the Lord."

"English man, English. My life depends on me understanding."

"Ok. Let me find another translation. Give me a sec. Here, I have found it in the New International Reader's version; the one who finds a wife finds what is good. He receives favor of the Lord." Preston held the receiver, while Garrison processed what he had just read to him.

Garrison let out a big sigh. "So, I am hearing God tell me that MJ is my good thing, my wife?"

"That is something you are going to have to come to terms with, on your own. I cannot tell you that MJ is your wife. I can tell you, if I heard God say those words, to me, that is what I would believe."

"So, MJ is my wife and I am favored of the Lord, because I have found her." Garrison stated, in a matter of fact tone. "Mary Jane Hall is my wife. Mary Jane Mitchell has a nice ring, wouldn't you say, my friend?" Garrison laughed out loud, as he asked the question.

"It has a wonderful ring to it." Preston smiled.

"Man, you are the first to know. I am going to propose to MJ, this weekend." Garrison sounded like a school boy, readying himself to ask his high school sweetheart to the prom.

"I am wishing you all the best, man. I am honored to be the first to hear it. I would love to be a fly on the wall, when you choose to pop the question." Preston mused.

"You will be more than that. I want you, Micah and Jeremiah to be there, too. This is monumental and I would love for my boys to be my moral support. You guys should have dates, as well, so MJ doesn't feel uncomfortable." Garrison's mind was racing. "Oh my goodness, I have to go out and get the perfect ring. Do you recommend a jeweler?"

"Well, there is Anderson & Wright Jewelers in Norfolk. It is on Waterside Dr. You know where that is, right? Preston asked.

"Yes, I know exactly where that is. Isn't it in the 300 block of Waterside Dr.?"

"You got it!"

"You have been a real friend, Preston. I don't know what I would have done had you not been available to speak to me. Yo, will you be my best man?"

"Of course, Garrison. I would love the honor of standing beside you when you take your vows. I am happy for you. Do you want me to tell Micah, since he is right in the building?"

"That would be great!" Garrison let out a big whoop, on the other end of the phone. "I am so pumped. I have been waiting for her and God has brought her back into my life."

"Awesome testimony."

"Yes, it is. Well, let me get off of this phone. I have work to do, here at the office and outside of the workplace."

The two friends hung up the phone, each to be lost in their own thoughts. Garrison to plan out the proposal and Preston to plan out how he was going to ask Damaris to be his date for the event.

CHAPTER ELEVEN

Damaris was preparing for Wednesday night service at Bread of Life. She looked forward to hearing Pastor Berry speak. She found his ability to expound on the Word of God, refreshing. She could sense the anointing, each time he opened the bible to bring forth his sermons. She has grown, so much, in the things of the Lord, under his spiritual care.

The telephone rang, just as she was putting on her make-up. She put down the brush and walked over to the phone, while wiping her hands on a towel.

"Hello."

"Hey girl, what's going on?" Ariel stated.

"I am getting ready for service. What about you?"

"I just got a call from Micah. He told me that his boy, Garrison, is going to propose to MJ."

"What?" Damaris shouted. "Oh my goodness, when did they hook up?"

"Well, you saw the two of them, when we met at the restaurant. Remember, they knew each other in high school and it seemed that they were attracted to each other, back then. Micah told me they got together, a few times, this past weekend being the last time, and hit it off. As it goes, Garrison called Preston to get some clarification about something he heard the Lord say while he had been praying. And the rest will be history, after this weekend, if she accepts his proposal."

"That has got to be the most bizarre reconnection, ever. How odd and wonderful, all at the same time. Everything is happening, so quickly, with them." Damaris was feeling a bit out of breath, as she thought of how this could happen. She had been working on freeing her mind from thoughts of Preston Lambert and perhaps God doing a quick work in a relationship between the two of them. With this happening with MJ and Garrison, her mind was reeling a mile a minute. She fought to focus on the topic, at hand.

"Well, that leads me to the reason for my call. Garrison wants his boys to be there when he pops the question." Ariel continued, "So, Micah was thinking that you and Preston could be paired off, at the dinner." Ariel waited.

Damaris could hardly believe her ears. Was she really hearing that she has another opportunity to meet with Preston? She felt like she was about to hyperventilate. She sat down on her bed. She felt ridiculous. She did not know Preston, like that, to be feeling giddy at the thought of seeing him, again.

Ariel cleared her throat. "Hello, over there. Are you willing to be Preston's date for the proposal, this weekend?"

"Did he ask for me to be his date?" Damaris inquired.

"Sort of. When he told Micah about the proposal and what Garrison wanted, he asked about my friends. So, Micah asked me to ask you. Now, I am asking you." Again, Ariel waited.

"Well, I do not want to appear forward, Ariel. How is that supposed to happen, if he has not asked for me to be his date?"

"Damaris, he asked about my friends. I know Preston was not thinking about Sela, because she is not his type. He had to be referring to you, on the sneak. So, if you agree, I will tell Micah. He will then make his move on Preston, give him your number and we will see what happens after that. Is that alright, with you?"

"I guess that will be alright." Damaris was feeling nervous. "Ariel, I do not want to come off like I need a hook up."

"Neither one of you want to come off, like you need a hook up. So, Micah and I are taking the matter into our own hands. No harm, no foul. Now, I have to get off of this phone and call Micah back to let him know he has the green light, from this end." The two of them said their goodbyes, and hung up the phone.

Damaris sat down on her bed to think about what had just transpired. She was about to find out if Preston Lambert found her interesting enough to spend more time getting to know her. What was she going to do, with herself, while she waited for a phone call that may never come? She hated feeling anxious about anything, so she decided to busy herself to get her mind off of the subject.

She returned to the bathroom, grateful for the distraction of preparation. She finished off her make-up, cleaned up the vanity and headed out the door for service.

As she drove, her mind wandered. She thought of Preston and how amazing it would be if they had a whirlwind relationship. They both loved the Lord, or so it appeared. God does not take a long time to speak, when the servant has listening ears. She left their first meeting intrigued. He had piqued her interest. She wanted to know more about him, however, did not want Ariel or Micah to think she was hard up and was sniffing out the first man who could hold a decent conversation. So, she had been left to wander and wonder through the subsequent weeks that has followed their initial encounter.

Now it was all coming to a head, so to speak. She would find out, within the next couple of days, whether Preston thought she was deep enough to delve further.

Damaris pulled into the parking lot of Bread of Life, found a parking spot, pulled in, turned the car off and sat for a moment. She needed to get her heart rate down to a pleasant resting speed. It seemed to be racing a mile a minute, as she drove from her house to the church. She needed to get herself, together. She was too grown and sophisticated to be driving herself to have a coronary over some man. However, Preston Lambert did not appear to be just any man. He was tall, handsome and he seemed so fit. His voice was a deep baritone, which resonated through her as he spoke. She imagined that voice, whispering in her ear, which caused a pang in the pit of her belly.

She, quickly, opened the car door and nearly ran into the house of the Lord. She needed God and she was not ashamed to do what was necessary to get her mind back.

CHAPTER TWELVE

Preston sat on the living room sofa for over an hour with the telephone, in his hand. Micah told him that Damaris goes to church on Wednesday evenings, so he did not want to call while she was in service. Nor did he want to seem overzealous and call as soon as he thought service ended. He contemplated waiting until tomorrow, but then that would be short notice, which could cause her to decline for lack of time. He berated himself for acting like an insecure man, desperate for companionship. He was assured that God had his wife picked out for him. He was just as certain that the Lord had placed a "knowing" sign, within his spirit which would signal him to move ahead. He felt his antennae being honed. However, he was not one to forge forward without careful consideration and prayer.

He had been praying as he sat with the telephone. He had asked God to give him a word, as He had done for Garrison. Yet, all he had was this sense of a raised awareness about Damaris. He wanted to know more about her. He wanted to spend time with her and allow the chips to fall where they may.

He knew he was attracted to her. He knew she was intelligent and had a sense of confidence about herself. She had a career that she loved, which implied that she was good at what she does. She was intrigued with his sense of spirituality, which told him that she was a God-fearing woman or at least wanted a man who was acquainted with God. The more he thought of her, the more he could sense his "feelers" perk up. Damaris Rhenay was an interesting woman who Preston would be proud to have on his arm.

He took a deep breath and dialed the number he had written down on a post-it note. He waited.

"Hello." Damaris answered.

"Hello, Damaris. This is Preston Lambert. We met, a couple of weeks ago…"

"Yes, I remember." Damaris had just pulled into her driveway when the phone call came though. She turned the car off, prior to answering.

Preston cleared his throat and continued. "I got your number from Micah, I hope you do not mind."

"I do not mind, at all. I am glad you called." She could not believe she spoke those words out of her mouth.

Preston breathed a sigh of relief. "Well, I am calling to see if you are busy, this weekend. I have been invited to dinner, by one of my longtime friends, and he stated I should bring a date. I realize we have met, just briefly, however I would like another opportunity to spend time with you."

"I would like that, very much." Damaris answered.

"Great! We are to meet everyone at Steinhilber's on Thalia Road in Virginia Beach. It is an upscale Italian restaurant. Do you like Italian food, Damaris?" He loved how her name sounded coming off of his lips.

Damaris could listen to him say her name, all evening. "I love Italian food, Preston." She just could not resist saying his name to hear how she sounded verbalizing it.

Preston was smiling, as he sat on the sofa. "I do, too. It seems like we have ourselves a date. I can pick you up, if you would like..." He allowed his sentence to trail off, hoping for her input.

"If you do not mind coming to pick me up, I do not mind riding with you. I live in Chesapeake, will that be an inconvenience for you?" Damaris asked.

"Just tell me where and I will be there."

"Let me know when you are ready and I will give you my address." Damaris stated. She waited until Preston acknowledged he had pen and paper, in hand. "2-6-5-3 North Elizabeth Harbor Drive. The zip code is 2-3-3-2-1, just in case you are using GPS."

"I appreciate the particulars. It should take me a less than thirty minutes to get to you, from my house. The restaurant closes at ten, so Garrison wanted to meet at seven. With that in mind, I would get to you around 6:15pm, if that works for you."

"I will be ready when you get here."

"So, it's a date. I will see you, on Saturday." He hung up the phone, after a quick good bye and leaned back on the sofa, with a smile of contentment on his face.

Damaris leaned back in the driver's seat of her 2009 Lexus IS 350C. She loved her car. It was bright red with white leather seats. She enjoyed the feel of the car. She saw the model before it hit the market. She decided, right then, that she would be the proud owner of one.

She sighed, and then opened the door to step out into the cool evening air. She was happy, in this moment. Did she dare to dream? What she knew she would do is pray. She did not want to be outside of the will of God. She was not about to start a relationship or even contemplate one, if it was not what God wanted for her life.

When she got to her porch, she sat down to pray. "Lord, I want what You want, plain and simple. I will listen for Your voice and I will obey. Please speak clearly, Father, so I can understand. I am Your sheep and You are my Shepherd. I am Your servant and You are my God. I do not want to waste my time, Preston's time or Your time following anything other than what You desire. I know You already know, so it will not take a long time. I just have to be still and listen."

Damaris sat on the steps for a long moment, before getting up and making her way into her home.

Preston sat praying, in that same moment. "Father, still my heart to hear You, in this matter. I do not want to overstep Your plan, in an attempt to create my own way. I want what You want and what You have prepared for me. I am Your willing and obedient servant. Speak to me, Lord, and show me the path You have for me. You have made me righteous and Your word says that the steps of a righteous man are ordered by You. I await Your marching instructions, in Jesus name. Amen."

He put the phone back on the receiver, turned out the lights in the living room and kitchen, then headed toward his bedroom. He was thinking of the time when he would be making his way to his marriage bed.

CHAPTER THIRTEEN

MJ was sitting on her bed, reading a book, when the telephone rang. It was Garrison, asking permission to come by in forty-five minutes. He missed her and wanted to see her face. She was excited and quickly assented to his request.

She contemplated changing her clothes, as she was in her favorite pajamas, however she thought against it. She did not want him to come over, at this hour, to find her fully dressed and made up. It would appear pretentious and MJ wanted to present herself in her truest form, so as not to build up false realities which she would not be able to maintain.

She walked into the living room and turned on the television set. She then moved into the kitchen to see what refreshments she had to offer, when Garrison arrived. There was some lemonade, orange juice, soda, water and half a bottle of white wine, in the refrigerator. She was satisfied with the variety and made her way back into the living room to sit in her favorite chair.

When the doorbell rang, she could feel her heart begin to race. She found herself excited about Garrison and what reconnecting with him could mean, since the moment she laid eyes on him in the restaurant a few weeks back. She remembered how attracted she was to him, while they were in high school and goose bumps raised on her arms. She relived the kiss and as it replayed in her mind, she recalled wanting more from him, in that moment. She, silently, thanked God for the interruption of friends because the kiss was taking her places, within herself, that were not suitable for the public eye.

MJ opened the door and stepped aside to allow Garrison entrance. She stood in the doorway and watched him walk into her home. She pressed her back against the door, in an attempt to catch her breath. She was amazed at the affect he had on her. He sat down on the sofa and looked in her direction and she felt a little apprehensive at how her body was responding to his gaze.

Garrison patted the seat, next to him. "Come sit with me." As he spoke, he seemed to look right through her.

MJ walked, slowly, across the room, never breaking the connection. He reached his hand out, as she approached, and pulled her onto his lap. She could feel him, as if there were no clothes between them. The heat was unbearable when he turned her face to his. "You are beautiful." His words were a soft whisper, in her ear and a chill ran down her spine.

The kiss that followed enveloped them in a blanket of desire. She felt his tongue gently probing her mouth and she could taste the mint flavored gum he had been chewing. Her eyes closed and she wrapped her arms around his neck, falling deeper and deeper into the kiss.

Garrison broke the embrace, abruptly, and carefully put MJ next to him on the sofa. "You take my breath way." His voice was husky with desire.

"I know the feeling." MJ responded. She knew she needed to change the subject, and fast, as things were getting too intense between them. She looked into Garrison's smoldering eyes and trembled.

"So, tell me what you have in the bag." She redirected, with a smile.

"Oh, I almost forgot about it. I brought dessert, for us to share. There is strawberry cheesecake in the bag. I hope you like it." He leaned in and kissed her, softly, on the lips. He sighed. "Nothing can taste as good as your lips."

"Mmmmm, take another taste." MJ reached up to kiss him, again.

"Delicious." He touched the nape of her neck and ran his finger across her skin. "We should get to eating the cheesecake, as other things are becoming more enticing."

MJ got up from the sofa and walked into the kitchen to get two saucers and forks. She returned to find Garrison standing by the patio doors.

"Do you mind having dessert out on the patio?" He asked.

"Of course not." She walked toward the doors and they walked out, together. He pulled out the chair next to the fire pit, allowing her to take her seat. He picked up the matches and started a fire.

MJ took the cheesecake and placed a slice on each saucer, along with a fork. Garrison pulled out a chair, for himself, and sat next to her.

"Tell me about your day, Garrison."

"Well, my day was spent thinking about you or working on not thinking about you, so I could get some work done. Everything I talked about, today was centered on you and recapturing lost time. I held a captive audience, as everyone is interested in regaining ground." He smiled, as he took a slice of cake into his mouth.

MJ looked on, mesmerized as she watched the cake go into his mouth. She was spellbound and intrigued at the mosaic of feelings she was experiencing at the sight. She wanted to be that slice of cheesecake.

Garrison looked up, with a concerned look on his face. "You sure you like cheesecake, MJ, because you are not touching yours. Should I have brought something, else?"

"I love cheesecake and I love watching you eat cheesecake." She picked up her fork, took a piece of the cake holding it out for Garrison to take. He leaned in, opened his mouth allowing the fork to slide into it, and then closed his lips around the cake. MJ's hands trembled as she gasped.

"Let's not play with fire, little vixen." Garrison stated, teasingly. "We will get burned."

Everything in MJ wanted to scream, *Let it burn, baby. Let it burn.* However, she resisted and blinked her eyes to refocus.

The couple ate their dessert, in silence. Garrison looked over at MJ and understood her fascination with food going into a person's mouth. His temperature was rising, with each forkful he watched her eat. MJ was lost in her thoughts of his mouth and what …

"So, tell me about your day at the Wellness Center." Garrison broke in and snapped her out of her fantasy.

"Well, I am working with overweight people who have committed to the 50 Million Pound Challenge, which was founded by Dr. Ian Smith. It is not just about people who find themselves grossly overweight, but who understand the health implications of holding onto the weight and who have made the decision to get healthy. As a nutritionist, I help them choose the best calories and food choices to assist them reach an attainable goal. Also, we work toward implementing the plan so it will benefit their communities and families. I love the freedom I am given by the director, Tamu Singletary. I love her and her vision for a holistic approach to healthcare."

"I see the trick to keeping us on the right track. All I need to do is get you to talking about your work. I witness a different fire, when you speak about what you do at the Wellness

Center. It is good to hear someone speak, so passionately, about the health and well being of others." Garrison was smiling.

"I am passionate about my work and the people who I am helping. My mother and grandmother were unhealthy eaters, thus their unhealthy physical states. When I was growing up I was determined not to allow myself to be another statistic in the African American community. I wanted to aid in the fight for healthy living."

"You always were taking up a righteous cause, even in high school. It is fantastic to know people can find career choices that are more of a calling than a job."

"Yes. I go to schools and speak with the students in an attempt to motivate them to dream. If we can reach them when they are young, there will be less unemployment or job dissatisfaction, as people will be moving into the field of their choice. As it stands, right now, most people are choosing jobs out of necessity. They need money, so they jump into the first position that will accept their resume."

"You got that right. So many of my fraternity brothers fell into the cycle of job seeking, rather than getting on a career path, and now they are stuck in positions they detest." Garrison sat back in his chair, as he spoke. "I had to cut those brothers loose, as they weren't about the drive to do more and be more than their parents. They did not avail themselves to all that James Madison University had to offer. They just focused on the partying and the carousing. Preston, Micah, Jeremiah and I weren't looking to return to the same neighborhood and do the same old things we saw them doing. So, we did what we had to do by speaking with the college counselors, looking to gain guidance for our futures." Garrison spoke with fervor. "We were determined not to be *that* brother on the corner, at thirty."

"I am impressed and grateful for your drive, Garrison. I saw it when we were in school and I can still see it. You were different from the other boys, which is what caused you to stand out. I took notice of you, because you dared to go against the grain of society."

"Thank the Lord for that, huh?" Garrison clapped his hands. "We would not have this opportunity had it not been for me using the good sense God gave me."

They laughed and finished their dessert. Afterward, MJ picked up the dishes and walked into the house to wash them. Garrison followed her after smothering the flame in the fire pit. He stood in the doorway of the kitchen, not giving in to his desire to walk up behind her and put his arms around her waist. They had barely averted trouble, earlier, he was not about to put them back into that predicament.

Once the dishes were washed and put away, the two walked back into the living room, as Garrison prepared to leave. They embraced and shared a brief kiss before he walked down the front steps.

"I enjoyed the visit, Garrison." MJ called after him, as he was getting into his car.

"As did I, my sweet." He replied. "Don't forget I will be picking you up at 6:00pm, Saturday. Put on something sexy."

Garrison started the car and backed out of the driveway. MJ stood in the door, waving, until he was out of sight. She closed the door and walked back into her bedroom.

CHAPTER FOURTEEN

Salester sat in her room, at her daughter-in-law's house. It was just before 5:00am and she could feel the unction to pray. Her mind recalled Kathleen's confession of the trouble she was having letting the thought of her husband's death become a reality. Her heart was heavy thinking about the turmoil she had been enduring, all these years, since the death of her son, Joseph.

They talked more, during the week, and Kathleen seemed to be walking out of the darkness. She noticed her sleeping in one of the guest rooms over the last couple of nights. She could only imagine her heartache when she made the decision to leave the bed she had shared with Joseph.

Salester encouraged her as best she could, however, Kathleen would need to call on the Lord for herself in order to make it through this trying time. She advised that she be patient with herself, as she made the transition from wife to widow. She noticed the pained expression at the mention of the word, *widow*, and the tears that welled up in her eyes.

This, too, shall pass; was all she could offer in consolation. There would be no easy button to push or magic pill to swallow that would smooth the rough road of recovery. It was not a journey where companions were welcome. It was a lonely path which no one wants to tread.

However, death is a certainty, if Jesus tarried. The devil wants those who remain, to feel like casualties of a war that God waged against mankind. His desire is to have people feel conflicted and confused about the death of their loved one. Instead, death is the doorway into eternity, as we have been created to eternal beings. Salester expressed this to Kathleen, on an evening that had been particularly difficult for her.

Mankind thinks of death as a curse or punishment, rather than a portal to their future. She expressed how loving God has been to His creation by allowing us to choose where we will spend eternity.

Too often, the human race struggle with the transition rather than welcome it. The body, in disease, attempts to rush the process and God sometimes chooses to relieve the sufferer by calling them to Himself. The work of death is a difficult one. The bereaved family should take the grieving period to reflect on the good times and wonderful memories that had been shared.

Rather, they choose to dread the future God has planned for them, as if He had not promised to walk with them through the valley of the shadow of death. He tells His children, fear no evil because He is with them.

Salester stood up and walked over to the picture window and sighed. She prayed for Kathleen and for all the grieving people, in the world. She prayed for their eyes to be opened and for them to recognize the comfort that God offers the mourner. She prayed for them to accept the morning's joy and mercy that is promised to those who weep. She interceded for those who did not know God, in the pardon of their sins because they would not be able to access the peace of God. She knew it to be real. She had to call upon it, when her husband and her son passed. She had an ache deep in the pit of her soul and she knew only God could deliver her from the torment she was feeling.

She walked the floor and she cried out to the God she knew for herself. She moaned, in her spirit, on behalf of those who could only moan while in the throes of abject misery. She allowed her spirit language to take over, as she could not put words to what was going on in her spirit. The tears flowed, freely, as she interceded for the widows and the orphans. She prayed until sweat appeared on her brow and she felt a release.

Kathleen lay sobbing, in bed, as she heard Salester praying in the other room. She had been awake for several hours begging God for relief. The pain and loneliness she felt every night had become unbearable. She wanted to be free from this longing she had for Joseph. She felt like he was an addiction that she needed to break free from, before she can be whole. She needed a fix and she needed the Lord to remove the taste, from her mouth.

She got up from the bed, realizing that she should be praying, as well. Mother Salester charged her to get before the Lord, for herself. She had not been expecting God to give her peace without Joseph. She did not want to feel good without her husband. She thought he deserved more than her and the children forgetting him. Yet, in her spirit, she acknowledged that this was not God's plan for her life. He did not want her to live in anguish and grief, over the loss of her love.

With all of the head knowledge that joy comes in the morning for those who weep during the night of their situation, Kathleen still felt the burden was more than she could shoulder. She groaned, deep within herself, because of the turmoil she was experiencing without Joseph by her side. She prayed, "Lord, all my desire is before You, and my groaning are not hid from You-my heart aches and my strength is failing. I put my trust in You, O God and I know You will answer me. I know Your thoughts and plans for my life are good. I do not know what You want from me or hope to gain by my losing Joseph, but I trust that You want what is best for me and there will be some good to come out of this horrible situation. Help me to find peace, Father, with Your purpose and plan."

The tears flowed freely down her cheeks and for the first time, in a long while, the agony did not accompany them. She felt as if her soul was being cleansed of the muck that had her bogged down for so long. She cried for what seemed an eternity, as she listen to Mother Salester continue to intercede.

She walked out of the bedroom, heading toward the bathroom, and she noticed Mother Salester coming out of her room. The two women walked toward one another and shared an embrace that spoke more than words.

CHAPTER FIFTEEN

White sand burned the soles of her feet, as she walked hand in hand with her lover, toward the water's edge. The cool feel of the blue liquid, tickled and refreshed their toes. A soft breeze wafted, playfully, by while seagulls sang their song, in the cloudless sky. The peace and serenity which surrounded her was surreal. She could never have imagined being this comfortable with anyone. Yet, here she was. She was basking in the revelry of being in love, with an amazing man. All of her praying and believing and waiting for God's approval had paid off, in a way that defied her imagination.

In that moment, she pinched herself, for fear she was dreaming. She turned her gaze to the man; her man. He had been smiling down at her reflection in the water, and then turned his attention to her face. Her heart swelled with adoration and gratitude, as she could see his affection for her in his eyes. It was palpable.

She felt unsteady and a little shy looking back at his intensity. She wanted to lower her gaze, but she was transfixed by the fire she sensed burning behind those beautiful hazel orbs.

He wrapped her in his arms and leaned down with his lips parted. She turned her face and mouth to meet his. The ensuing kiss seemed to cause the water to boil, as she felt the flames of passion course through her body and into her feet. Her breath seemed to fail her, as she felt suffocated with desire. The kiss intensified, buckling her knees. He held her, fast, to keep her from falling to the ground ...

The blaring alarm startled Damaris. So much so, her heart was racing and her hands were trembling. The effects of the dream transcended fantasy, reaching into reality as her body ached for the touch of the man in her dream. She could feel perspiration on her brow and top lip. Her skin felt hot, yet goose bumps appeared, as if she were chilled.

She reached for the glass of water that had been on her nightstand and took a sip, in an attempt to calm her. She took another sip, and then downed the remaining water. She wondered what would help her fevered body. Damaris could not remember a dream having this affect on her, in the past. She wondered, briefly, who the man could have been. It was not long, before her mind's eye reminisced and recaptured the face of the mystery man. It was Preston Lambert.

She felt embarrassed, sitting in bed alone. She could feel her cheeks flush and her eyelids lower, in shame. "Lord, what am I going to do?" She spoke aloud, hoping for an audible and quick answer. Her inquiry was met with silence.

She threw back the covers and swung her feet to the floor. Her nightgown was soaked and her sheets were especially ruffled. She let out a huff and jumped out of bed, walking into her bathroom, while discarding her nightclothes, as if they offended her.

As she prepared her bath, her mind raced in several directions, at once. How would she ever be able to face Preston, tonight, after having such a fiery dream of him? She was certain it would be all over her face, while they sat next to one another during the ride to the restaurant. She, even, imagined everyone would be able to see it on her face, as they sat at the table.

In an irrational moment, she contemplated calling Preston and coming up with an excuse as to why she could not accompany him to dinner. She quickly, dismissed the idea, as that may affect a memorable night for her friend. She was in a quandary.

She needed to think. She wanted to be level-headed and calm. Yet, she felt anything, but collected. She was panicking, thinking about being in close proximity with a man that she had such a vivid and passionate dream. She remembered Preston saying it could take up to forty-five minutes to get to Steinhilber's. How was she going to act or *react* in such tight quarters, with him, for nearly an hour?

Damaris slid into the tepid bathwater. She leaned her head back against her bath pillow and closed her eyes. She sighed, deeply, as she willed her mind to focus on anything except Preston. She squeezed her lids, tightly, hoping for the visions to cease. The water felt like caresses upon her skin. The pillow felt like his hand behind her head. The bath oil took on a musky scent, like masculine cologne.

She berated herself and her body for betraying her, as she opened her eyes, reached for the soap and wash cloth. This bath would not be the thing to relax and soothe her overactive imagination.

Just as she stepped out of the tub and toweled off, the phone rang. She contemplated letting the voicemail pick up, then decided against it. She wrapped the towel around her and trotted out of the bathroom, to catch the call before the ringing ended.

She reached the receiver, just in time, only to wish she had listened to her first instinct. "Hello Preston."

CHAPTER SIXTEEN

Preston had been pacing the floor, of his bedroom, for thirty minutes before deciding to give Damaris a call. Now, he wished he had not. The voice which greeted him on the other end, sounded annoyed, almost disappointed.

"Hello Damaris. I am sorry to bother you at such an ungodly hour. However, I just wanted to insure that you had a good rest of your week and to see if we were still on for this evening." He could not believe he mustered up the courage to state his real intent for the call. "I hope I have not caught you at a bad time. I sense a note of exasperation in your voice." He found no reason to back up, now.

"I am sorry, Preston." Damaris tried to quiet the butterflies that had taken flight in her belly. She felt hot and she wanted to kick herself for allowing her emotion to be heard. "I was just getting out of the bath and I was rushing to get to the phone. Please do not think my tone had anything to do with your call." *However, it had everything to do with you*, she thought to herself. She sat down on the bed, cradled the phone in her shoulder, so she could continue to dry off.

"Forgive me, for disturbing you. I can call you back..." He began.

"No, no, no. It is quite alright." Damaris hurried. She felt the tension, in her body quell as she listened to his voice. It brought her a sense of calm, along with the fire. It was like an inferno, inside of an ice castle; oddly tranquil. "I am glad you called, actually." She heard herself saying, as she lay back on the bed.

"Are you? Is everything alright?" Preston began to get a tinge of nervousness.

"Everything seems to oddly be quieting down, now that I am speaking with you. I had a disturbing dream which I could not shake. As hard as I tried, nothing worked, until I heard your voice." What was she saying? Why would she give him that power over her; to know that he calmed her?

There was concern, in his voice, along with a bit of intrigue. "I am sorry to hear that your morning was not bathed in the sunshine that washes over the sky, today. On the other hand, I am thrilled to know that I have contributed to your ease. For some reason, that brings me a sense of happiness; knowing that I can do that for you." Preston walked out onto the deck, in his backyard and took a seat by the fire pit. As he sat, he felt a stirring in his spirit.

"Damaris, will you mind if I pray for you?" Preston asked, as he put his feet up.

She was taken aback, at the request. "Of course, I do not mind. I would be a fool to turn down prayer. If God is leading you to pray for me, Preston, please do not hesitate. You do not, even, have to ask." Damaris felt the Holy Spirit, within her, quicken her spirit. This was right.

Preston began, "Father, I come to You, this morning, on behalf of my sister, Damaris. Only You know what she is experiencing and what is causing her concern. Lord, I pray that You give her peace, in her inner man. Let her feel Your presence, in the midst of her test. You are her Shepherd; lead her through this moment she is encountering today. Smile into her situation, letting her know that You are pleased with her willingness to come to You for comfort. I thank You, God, for allowing me to be the one to pray for her, at this time. Whatever the circumstance, let her know that You are working together, within it, to cause good to come out of it. You desire for her to be free from concern, therefore, You have taken her burdens and her cares and placed them on Your Son. She can walk and conduct her affairs, knowing that her steps are ordered by You and that Your righteousness overshadows any inadequacy. Bless her, my God. Bless her home, her job, her family and her friends. Speak to her heart and give her clear instructions, causing calm and tranquility to reign in her members. In the name of Jesus, I come to You; Amen."

There was a moment of silence, on the phone, as the two of them communed with God, in their own way. Both could feel the Presence of God coming into their respective settings, causing a moment of reverence and worship. Preston could hear a slight sniffle, on the other end of the phone and his heart warmed. *Lord, she is a woman of worship who has an intimate relationship with You,* Preston spoke within his heart. At that moment, God spoke to him in the most audible voice he could remember experiencing. Then, the tears began to fall from his eyes.

Damaris sat, as her tears flowed freely from her eyes. She sensed the Holy Spirit speaking directly to her heart, as Preston prayed. There was a feeling of familiarity as he called out to God, on her behalf. There was a knowing, within her, that this would not be the last time he would pray for her. She felt her respect blossom, for this man of prayer. It grew into a garden of admiration and gratitude for God allowing their paths to cross. She heard the voice of the Lord, calling out to His bride.

"Yes, Father," was the whispered reply from both Preston and Damaris, in unison.

CHAPTER SEVENTEEN

Ariel sat, quietly, in the passenger seat of Micah's Infinity QX56. She loved the deep, rich garnet color of the exterior, the graphite leather seats and the wood trim. She remembered squealing like a school girl, when he drove up to take her for a spin. As she stared out of the window, her thoughts raced by as quickly as the scenery.

She was trying to identify the emotions she was experiencing, during the dinner for Garrison and MJ. She watched the guests of honor fawn all over each other, after MJ accepted his proposal. There were meaningful looks, brief kisses and lingering touches shared between the two. She didn't want to admit it, but she felt a bit envious. Their passion was evident, in every action. Something she never identified in her relationship with Micah. Sure, there was love between the two of them; however, she never experienced what she was witnessing between Garrison and MJ.

She attempted to avert her attention, as much as she could, however, she noticed there was something going on between Preston and Damaris, as well. She wasn't able to pinpoint it, exactly, but there was something she did not expect to see. There was a deeper connection, a certain knowing in their communication, that one would not expect in a mere second meeting.

Ariel watched the two of them, intently. She was certain nothing had transpired between them, physically. She was sure that Damaris would have shared that information. She wondered when there was time for this connection to build and for it to be visible to onlookers.

As they drove, in silence, Ariel could feel discontentment rising from the pit of her belly. Why couldn't she have such a connection, in her relationship, with Micah? She turned to look at the man she loved. Could the casual observer note a deep and meaningful attachment between the two of them? She scoffed, in her mind, how could they when it wasn't evident to her and she was in the relationship.

She and Micah were much like the verse in a song, 'easy like Sunday morning.' They were comfortable, with each other, and that felt good to her. Up until now, she had been satisfied with the way things were between them. There was, virtually, no sexual pressure which kept her free from the thought of slipping up. Yet, tonight, she wondered if that was a sign that something was just a little askew with her. She found Micah very attractive. He was attentive and caring. He was hard working and wanted her to have the best things, in life. He loved her, of that she was certain and felt secure.

Ariel reached over and placed her hand on Micah's free one. She felt the strength in his grip, as he held her hand, in his own. She waited for the fire. However, she was disappointed when all she felt was peaceful. She lifted his hand to her lips and kissed it, gently. She watched a smile cross Micah's lips, but there was no longing in his eyes. As a matter of fact, there was nothing stirring her, either. She decided she needed to investigate her suspicions, further. She took his finger and placed in her mouth, and gently sucked on it, waiting for a sensual reaction from either of them. Instead, she felt foolish and Micah looked over, confused.

"What is going on?" Micah asked, as they stopped at a traffic light. "You have been unusually quiet, since dinner, and now you are licking my fingers."

She dropped his hand, feeling rejected. "Micah, do you want me?"

Micah furrowed his brow, as he turned the corner. "Where is this coming from, Ariel? Of course, I want you. There should be no doubt, in your mind. I have been working hard to get this promotion, in an attempt to make our lives, together, comfortable."

"I am not asking you if you want to *be* with me, Micah. I want to know if you desire me, sexually." She turned her body, to face him.

Micah paused. "Is this some sort of trick question?" He pulled his truck into Ariel's driveway and turned off the engine.

Ariel sighed. "It is not a trick question, Micah. I am never looking to trick you. I really want to know if there is some sort of sexual tension between the two of us." There was a pleading look, in her eyes.

Micah turned to face her. "Baby, of course I want you. How could I not? You are beautiful...gorgeous, even. I find you, very sexy."

A tentative smile began to cross Ariel's lips. "Really?"

"Oh yes." Micah leaned over, taking her face into his hands and placed a gentle kiss, on

Ariel's forehead. He kissed both of her eyelids, her cheeks, then finally her mouth.

"Are you going to come in, before you head home?" Ariel questioned. She felt a strange sensation begin to spread throughout her body. She wanted to investigate it, further.

"Of course. Give me a moment to come around and open your door." He turned off the ignition and stepped out of the truck, quickly making his way to the passenger side.

As he opened the door, Ariel swung her legs out and her skirt moved high up her leg. The cool night breeze caused chill bumps to rise on her skin. Micah's hands slid up her legs and rested on her thighs.

"Your legs are cold." He offered, as he stroked her skin. "Let me warm them for you."

Ariel did not move; she was enjoying the sensation of Micah's warm hands on her cool skin. She watched his hands caress her thighs, then travel back down her legs to her calves. Without thinking, she raised her skirt higher. Micah looked up to see the white lace panties she was wearing.

"What are we doing, Ariel?" Micah questioned.

Ariel placed one finger on her lips, to quiet his inquiry. She placed her hand on his, and pulled it up to her breast. She felt like she was having an out of body experience. This was not something she was accustomed to doing and was uncertain where it all was coming from, at this moment. What she did know was that she enjoyed the feelings that coursed through her body.

"Are you sure, this is what you want, Ariel?" Micah felt compelled to get assurance.

"I have never been more sure of anything, Micah." She slipped her panties off, right in front of him, in the driveway of her home.

Micah climbed into the truck and closed the door. Ariel pushed the seat back to its furthest position, and then moved so Micah could take her seat. He unbuckled his belt and unzipped his slacks. Ariel slipped off her shirt, exposing the matching bra to her panties. As she lifted her skirt, to sit on Micah's lap, she gasped at his size.

"I will not hurt you, Ariel." Micah breathed out. He reached for her hips and gently pulled her onto himself. He wrapped his arms around her back, as she leaned onto his chest. They kissed, deeply, and Micah groaned throwing his head back onto the seat.

Immediately, Ariel knew what happened and disappointment flooded her body. Was this what she had been waiting for, the whole time? Was it supposed to end this quickly, without her getting a chance to enjoy any of it? She looked into Micah's eyes and saw his embarrassment. He turned away, as he quickly removed her from his lap. He jumped out of the truck, adjusting his pants.

Ariel replaced her shirt and stepped out of the truck while smoothing her skirt. She placed her panties, in her purse, as Micah closed the passenger side door. He walked her to the door, murmured what sounded like an apology, then hurried back to the truck and drove away.

She stepped inside her foyer, closed the door behind her and cried. Guilt flooded her body, as quickly as the longing had, in Micah's truck. There was no reason for her to have allowed her jealousy of Garrison and MJ, cause her to sin against her relationship with God. She knew better. Conviction coursed through her spirit, like a hot branding iron. She felt dirty and cheated, all at the same time. Sex was for the marriage bed, not for the front seat of an SUV.

And for what, she wondered. There was no deep-seated satisfaction; in fact, there was a great sense of dissatisfaction.

"Flee fornication! Flee fornication! Flee fornication!" Ariel slapped her forehead and screamed out into the empty house. Her voice echoed into the quiet rooms. Torment was wreaking havoc in her mind. How could she face Micah, again? She was not the woman he thought she was, anymore. She felt cheap and childish. Was this why the bible spoke against covetousness? Did it cause people to go against their beliefs to chase another person's life? It certainly caused her to lay aside her convictions, in search of a passion she saw in another couple's eyes.

"I am a wretch!" She yelled out, as she felt sin's evidence running down her legs.

CHAPTER EIGHTEEN

Micah berated himself the whole ride home. There was no reason he should have allowed himself to lose control, like some school boy. He felt the Holy Spirit caution him, yet he just rolled along, as if he had no relationship with God, at all. No excuse could vindicate him, right now. He had cried out to God, when he was out of Ariel's driveway. However, he had to reflect and wonder if he did so because of his embarrassment in how quickly it was over. He wonders if he would have taken the express route to God, if things had gone better or longer? He cringed, just thinking about the moment. How could he face Ariel, again? Would she trust him to take care of all of her needs, once they were married?

Thoughts of inadequacy plagued his mind, as he drove to his home. In the midst of his turmoil, he contemplated going back and doing it right. His pride did not want him to go out, like that. He was a man! He knew how to handle a woman. He was not some novice, with little experience. He had several sexual relationships, prior to his decision to do the right thing by God and save himself for his wife. He wanted her to know that he would be able to take care of her, in every way. He banged his head, on the steering wheel, while at the traffic light. Of course, he could not straighten out the situation until he did what was respectable and marry her.

He wasn't sure what had gotten into Ariel, this evening. He wanted to blame her for what happened, however, he chose to be the mature male and take full responsibility. He could have averted the entire situation, as he had done in the past with other females. Yet, in his mind it was not the same thing. Ariel was not just a random chick, on the side. She is the woman he planned on spending the rest of his life with; she is to be the mother of his children. He entertained the idea of this being the reason he conceded with the act that transpired this evening.

He needed to get before the Lord and to his accountability partner, Preston. He knew his buddy would be disappointed and may have some choice words for him, but he could not hide his sin. The bible asserts that believers should confess their faults one to another. Micah knew this was not for gossip's sake, but to keep the saints from covering up what could keep the rest of the Body from succeeding. One member of Christ's church is not an island in and of themselves. Everyone's actions affect the whole, just as much as the physical body feels the pain of a stubbed toe or a broken bone.

So, Micah decided he would go into his office, pull out his favorite study bible and call out to the Lord, in abject desertion of his sin; knowing he would find grace and mercy to face another day. His spirit felt the conviction of God's Holy Spirit and his soul was broken. Reparation was necessary and he refused to let another moment go by, without doing his part.

He was reminded of a Greek word, which he learned while taking psychology in college. Carl Jung's use of the word *Metanoia* asserts it is the spontaneous attempt of the psyche to heal itself of unbearable conflict by melting down and then being reborn in a more adaptive form. In theology, it is the same word used for repentance. At this moment, he completely identified with the two being one and the same. Sin and righteousness cannot reign in the same body – the conflict, while trying to serve two masters, causes grief of spirit and the soul breaks down in order to adapt to one or the other. In his case, he would choose right standing with God over the fleeting pleasure of sin. Micah flinched, inwardly, at the pun.

CHAPTER NINETEEN

Damaris loved driving when she felt the need to think and clear her mind. She jumped on Interstate 664 toward Virginia Beach, accelerated to sixty-five miles per hour, and then set the cruise control. The soulful sound of Wynton Marsalis' trumpet filled the car with blues intones. She took a deep breath and settled in for the ride.

She had hoped she could talk with Ariel about it all, however she was unable to reach her for days. In fact, she hadn't spoken with her, since the dinner for MJ and Garrison. The recorded message on her answering machine informed Damaris that she was a bit under the weather and wasn't taking calls. So, she didn't want to drop in and disturb her with her frivolity.

Preston had called, every day, since their date. The conversations were brief, yet they caused her a sense of joy. He asked of her day and shared the highlights of his day, with her. The talks left her wanting to learn more about the man that God spoke to her about, with pristine clarity. She was unclear as to what she was supposed to do with the information, thus the need for this ride.

She pressed the push to talk button, on her dashboard, then used the speed dial number for Ariel. She was beginning to become concerned. Preston advised she had not been to work, all week, and Micah was unable to reach her either. Damaris listened, as the phone rang and rang, until the answering machine picked up.

"Ariel, this is Damaris, again. I am getting concerned, so I am going to come over this evening with some egg drop-wonton soup and some ginger tea. I will, also, rent Sisterhood of the Traveling Pants video for our viewing pleasure. So, do not …" The sound of the buzz blared in her ear, cutting her off.

"Hello." Ariel answered. There was the sound of recent crying, in her voice, and sniffling in the background.

"Sweetie, what is the matter?" Alarm and concern registered in Damaris' voice. She looked around for the nearest exit, and then turned on her blinker, to make her move to the ramp. "I am on my way, right now. I will forego the soup and tea."

"I am not sure I have the strength to eat or talk, Damaris." A fresh flow of tears began to fall, as Ariel spoke.

"We do not have to talk, if you do not want to, Ariel. Or I will listen as long as you need me, if you choose you are ready." Damaris looked in the rearview mirror, as she changed lanes to make the turn into Ariel's subdivision. She was grateful that she had not gotten further into her trip. She rounded the corner, too quickly, and had to overcorrect in order to miss hitting a parked car.

"You don't have to, Damaris. I just answered the phone because I did not want you to worry." Ariel moved the phone, so she could blow her nose.

"Of course, I have to come, girl. Open the door, I will be there in less than two minutes." Damaris advised.

"Okay." Ariel managed, just before hanging up the phone.

Damaris pushed the talk button, to end the call, as she turned into Ariel's driveway. She pressed the ignition button to turn off the car, as she was opening the door. After grabbing her bag, she stepped out of the car and walked onto the porch. She reached for the handle, just as Ariel opened the front door.

When the two friends saw each other, both began to cry. They embraced for a long time, before either was ready to let go. Ariel and Damaris walked hand in hand, into the living room, and sat down on the plush rug which was in front of the fireplace.

Damaris noticed there was an empty box of tissues, on the floor and a small trash can filled with the discarded ones. She could sense depression in the air and immediately began to pray, in the Spirit, quietly. There were no telltale signs to give her a clue as to what had taken place to cause her childhood friend to sink into this dark place. Concern etched her brow, however she remained silent, as promised.

There were hushed cries, as Ariel laid her head in her friend's lap. She was grateful for the comfort she felt, while Damaris rubbed her head. How could she tell her what she had done? How was she ever going to come to terms with the sin she had committed? If she had cast down the vain imaginations, in their infancy, as she sat during dinner, coveting Garrison and MJ's fiery connection, it would have been an easier fix. Yet, she entertained the thoughts, gave them life with her focused attention and it produced a death (of sorts) in her spirit man. There was a major disconnect between her and God, that fateful night. She made herself and her desires an idol, by putting them before the knowledge of God. She magnified lust, instead of the word of God that rested on the inside of her. She allowed her mind to fix itself on a perceived goal, instead of keeping it on God; therefore, she lost her peace. Ariel felt tormented, day and night. She could not rest, as she had nightmares of hell's fire ravaging her sin-sick soul.

Damaris heard Ariel whimper and her body tremble. She looked down and saw her eyes looking wild, as tears fell freely down her cheeks. "What is it, Ariel? What has happened? You can tell me. I want to help you, sweetie." She pleaded. Her only response was a shaking head and more tears.

"There is nothing too hard for God, Ariel. He can take whatever is troubling you and work it out. In fact, He has already made provision and a way for you to escape what has attached itself to you." Damaris was certain that an unhealthy spirit had made its abode, within the confines of the walls of her best friend's home. She could sense it, deep within herself.

"Has someone hurt you?" She spoke, softly.

Silence was her reply.

"It's okay, sweetie. We will just sit here, as long as you want." Damaris continued to pray.

Ariel grabbed a tissue from a new box and blew her nose, after wiping her eyes. She tossed it into the little trash can, then laid her head back on Damaris' lap, allowing her to soothe her brow with her cool hands.

Damaris began to recite the twenty-third psalm, as she had learned it from the New International version of the bible. "The Lord is my Shepherd, I shall not be in want. He makes me lie down in green pastures, He leads me beside quiet waters, He restores my soul. He guides me in paths of righteousness for His name's sake. Even though I walk through the valley of the shadow of death, I will fear no evil for You are with me; Your rod and Your staff they comfort me. You prepare a table before me in the presence of my enemies. You anoint my head with oil; my cup overflows. Surely goodness and love will follow me all the days of my life, and I will dwell in the house of the Lord forever."

The evening turned into night, as the two women sat, together. Damaris did not move, as

Ariel stretched out with her head still on her lap. "Do you need me to get you something, sweetie?"

"No." Ariel answered, as she closed her eyes. "I want to sleep, Damaris. Will you stay, so I can sleep?" There was a pleading, in her voice, which caused sorrow to flood her heart.

"Of course, I will stay, Ariel. I will stay as long as you need me."

Before long, Damaris heard the soft, even breathing of sleep overtake her friend. She reached onto the couch for the blanket and placed it on Ariel. She pulled a nearby chair, close, so she could lean against the back to support herself. She knew she would be there for the night.

Damaris was startled awake, with the loud cries of Ariel. "I am sorry, God! I am sorry! Will you ever forgive me, Lord? How can you forgive me, when I cannot forgive myself?"

"Ssshhhh, sweetie. Hush now. It is alright. You were having a bad dream." Damaris rocked Ariel in her arms, attempting to comfort her.

"What am I going to do?" Ariel asked. "What am I going to do? How can I face him, again?"

"Who, baby?" Damaris inquired.

"I don't know if I can ever face anyone, again. I am not sure why you are not disgusted, just looking at me. I can't, even look at myself." Tears began to stream down, afresh.

"I cannot help you or answer your questions, without knowing what you are talking about, Ariel. Do you want to tell me?" Damaris waited.

"I cannot bring myself to mouth the words. I am a despicable wretch." Ariel spit the words out, as if they were bitter gall.

"Is this a situation between you and Micah? I, only, ask because he has been asking Preston to see if I have heard from you. All I could tell him was what everyone who attempted to call you knew ... that you were not feeling well and not taking calls. He is worried about you, Ariel. We all are." Damaris concluded.

"Micah seems fine?" Ariel queried.

"From the little that Preston has said, I did not ascertain that there was anything the matter with Micah. Did you guys have a fight?"

Again, tears and silence were her answer.

This is going to be a long night, Damaris thought, as Ariel laid her head back upon her lap.

~~~~~~~~~~~~~~~~~

The sound of a ringing phone could be heard in the distance and Damaris wondered why no one would answer it. She awakened, quickly, as Ariel's answering machine picked up and the sound of her voice filled the room. After the beep, Micah's voice could be heard, as he left a message "Ariel, please pick up. We need to talk."

Damaris looked down, thinking Ariel was still asleep, only to find her wide awake. "Sweetie, Micah sounds so worried. Whatever is going on, between the two of you, will never get resolved as long as you avoid him. You should not allow this thing to continue to take up residence in your home and heart, any longer."

Ariel knew her friend was right. She had locked herself away from the world, for a week. She had not gone to church or work, since her and Micah had had sex. She winced, as she thought about it. Why did she not wait to be made love to, on her wedding night, as she had planned her entire life? Instead, she opted for sin's pleasure in a sex act; except there was no pleasure.

"God loves you, Ariel. You can depend on His love to draw you from the miry clay of depression that has grasped your soul. His perfect love will cast out the fear of rejection or abandonment. He will never leave you, nor forsake you – that is His promise and He is not slack concerning His promises. He is not man that He should lie to you. I know all of this is not new to you, however sometimes it needs to be heard. If you need to repent, then find your place in His mercy and go to Him knowing He will not cast you aside. You are His beloved. You are engraved on the palms of both of His hands, and nothing or no one can snatch you out, not even yourself. Go to God, Ariel. Do not treat Him like a judgmental human. He will not cast you away, if you come to Him seeking restoration." Damaris knew she was on to something, as Ariel's eyes glazed over, again.

Damaris took Ariel's hands into her own, as she felt lead to pray for her friend: "Most Gracious God, my Father - I come to you, today, giving you all the honor and glory due your name. You are the Master of the universe - Sovereign ruler of all of the heavens and earth. You sit high and you look low, forever concerning yourself with your creation. You own the cattle on a thousand hills and you have stored up riches and possessions for your children to inherit, if we just believe. I make your name great, in the earth. I will always declare your awesome wonders to all who will listen. You intend to manifest your blessings and favor upon your people, your chosen ones - the apple of your eye - You have us engraved on the palms of both your hands, never to leave or forsake us. Your mercy is from everlasting to everlasting - and your grace encompasses us, like a robe - You have crowned us with your loving kindness and encamped us round about with ministering angels, like flames of fire. It is by your command that the sun rises and sets - You declare when the tide rolls in and goes out - at your word, the moon shines brilliantly upon the earth - You are magnificent! You are awesome! You are marvelous - everything you do, is for our good - and I thank you for it all. I come to you, Elohim, on behalf of my sister - I declare that your greatness is made manifest in her life - I decree that your glory will surround her, like a cloud, being evident to those around her. The ministry, you have called her to, is blessed. You have fallowed out the ground, therefore as she walks she prospers and increases - You have brought increase to those she has been allowed to plant and to those she has been allowed to water - she is a fruitful garden, with leaves upturned in worship. Bless her with longstanding endurance like the palm tree - allow her to flourish and be continually verdant, like the evergreen - let her words be soft and filled with power and beauty, like the rose - Touch her, with your love, and cause her to bow her heart in adoration as her face shines with your grace. Cause her to allow your Spirit to search her heart, her mind and her spirit, turning over every area to you, in submission to your will for her life. Speak to her, on her bed, at night - greet her with your Presence, when she awakes, in the morning - walk with her in the cool of the evening - Woo her, Adonai! Draw her to yourself and hold her close, when she cries out to you - Be fierce in your protectiveness, causing her peace as she walks through any valley - she shall fear no evil, because you are with her - comfort her, console her, build her up in her most holy faith. Come into her situations, circumstances and her immediate personal space, as she communes with you - Let your Spirit surround her, on all sides, infusing her with power, might, strength and security. She is NEVER alone. Speak to her heart, right now. Make clear your plans for her "right now" season. Still her heart, so she can hear your whispers of direction - Light her way, as she leads those you have called her to lead - Help her to submit to whom you have called to mentor and lead her. She is your daughter and you are her Father - blow your wind upon her, right now, in the name of Jesus and pull her onto your lap - allow her to lay her head upon your bosom, to quiet her spirit. Lull her into the sweet sleep that you have designed for your beloved, at night - Refresh and revive her for the day's journey, in the morning. She is healed, by the stripes of Jesus - any sickness or disease that tries to attach itself to her, is trespassing and has no right - She is free, because Jesus, your Truth, has made her free - The enemy has no power over her, her ministry, her family or her friends - his assignment is loosed from her life and bound with the shackles, from heaven - She will walk, daily, in the Light and power of your Love. I pray this and believe it to be done, according to the power you have given to me - by the name of your Son, Jesus - it is so - AMEN!" Tears fell from Damaris' eyes and down her cheeks, as she looked at her friend.

Damaris' voice was filled with emotion. "After you have cleared the air, with the Father, clear the air with your man. He loves you and nothing that has transpired between the two of you will ever change that. You know Micah loves himself some Ariel." She smiled toward her friend and was pleased to see a small smile creep up on her face.

"That a girl! Now, we need to get up off of this floor, pick up around the house, open the shades and windows and get something in your belly." Damaris got up and walked toward the kitchen, as Ariel picked up things in the living room.

"I am going to whip you up one of my famous omelets, before I head home to shower and change."

CHAPTER TWENTY

Preston sat with his mother and grandmother, as Pastor Robert Howard expounded on a sermon he entitled, 'Be Encouraged.' He nodded, at Micah, who was seated across the aisle.

"We serve an awesome God!" Pastor Howard began. "He sits high and looks low. He is acquainted with our every move and our every thought. He has provided for our every need, before we were yet formed in our mother's womb. He is Sovereign and He is aware of every situation that confronts us. By the stripes of Jesus, we stand healed, delivered and set free from anything that tries to attach itself to our bodies."

Micah was engrossed, from the very beginning. He had spent much time, before the Lord, this week. He needed to hear and encouraging word, today.

"We stand, in faith, awaiting the manifestation of health and healing. We are blessed and no plague can come nigh our dwelling. We are the head and not the tail. We are above, only, and not beneath. We are heirs and joint-heirs with Jesus Christ and partakers of the Abrahamic Covenant. We are the Apple of God's eye, beloved and called peculiar treasures."

There were 'amens' and 'say it Pastor', from the congregation, as he exhorted the people with the promises of God.

He continued, "We are fearfully and wonderfully handcrafted by God. Each of us is unique and expertly taken care of by our Father. Our spirits bear witness with His Holy Spirit, therefore we can cry, "Abba, Father."There is no attack that comes at us that God has not provided for our rescue. We can quench every fiery dart of the enemy, with our shield of faith (the substance of things hoped for and the evidence of things not seen). When faced with hardships, we are given the opportunity to see just what we are made of and/or where we need to bulk up on our skills. We are overcomers, because greater is He that is in us, than he that is in the world. Children of God, we were created in the image and the likeness of the Godhead ... we possess a supernatural creative ability, which lies in our words."

Preston was trying to remain focused on what Pastor Howard was speaking. His life was changing and God had informed him, beforehand. Damaris Rhenay was a kindred soul and God has seen fit to include her in his circle. He needed to speak with his mother, after church, today. She would be able to help him make sense of what he heard and how he should govern the next steps of his life.

The pastor's voice broke through his musing. "I speak life. I speak strength. I speak provision. I speak health. I speak joy, which is your strength. I speak peace. I speak abundance in your spiritual, as well as your natural life. You are blessed, to be a blessing. Let patience have her perfect work, in you. You are loved by an awe inspiring God! He is faithful and just. He is love and He has shed that love abroad in our hearts. As we confess our sins, He is faithful and just to forgive our sins and to cleanse us from all unrighteousness. Your sins and mine have been tossed into the sea of forgetfulness ... as far as the east is from the west, so far has He removed our transgressions from us."

Micah stood up, clapping his hands and shouting out in praise. He was so grateful for God's forgiving nature. He was appreciative of the Lord granting him a stay of execution, for his sins. He was desperate to walk in forgiveness.

"He gives seed to the sower and bread to the eater. As we keep our hearts and minds set on His kingdom and His righteousness ... all of our needs are met. We have no reason to take thought for what we shall eat or what we shall drink or what we shall wear ... He knows. We have no reason to be anxious or to fret ... JUST TRUST HIM!" Pastor Howard pounded on the pulpit for effect.

The congregation was on their feet praising God. There were members who walked up to the front, placing a seed on the altar, acknowledging they had heard God for their situation.

"Now unto Him Who is able to keep you from falling ... who can do exceedingly, abundantly above what we can ask or even think ... who blesses according to His riches in glory, by Christ Jesus ... BE BLESSED!" He closed his bible and he made his way down from the pulpit.

Pastor Howard called to those who had never acknowledged their need for Christ. He beseeched the backslider to return. He invited others to join the local assembly by the name of El Shaddai Worship Center, of which he was the leader. He called for the persons who wanted to be filled with the Holy Spirit, with the evidence of speaking in tongues.

Several people made their way to the front of the church to be prayed over, counseled and to give their information as new members.

After service ended, Micah made his way over to Pastor Howard. "Excuse me, Pastor. May I have a moment of your time?"

"Of course, you may, son. What can I do for you?" Pastor Howard was of medium build and height. His salt and pepper hair was cut low to his head. His skin was the color of special edition chocolate and was flawless. Many would call him handsome, including his wife, First Lady Adell, which stood nearby. "Excuse me, honey."

The two men walked toward the right of the pulpit, where they could have a modicum of privacy. "Well, I would love to have a meeting with you, as it pertains to my long-time girlfriend, Ariel and I. I have sought the Lord and believe it is time to ask her to marry me."

Pastor Howard patted Micah on the back, heartily. "Praise the Lord, son; that is incredible news. God loves covenant, in all forms, especially if He is in the mix. I will have my secretary, Abigail, check my calendar and set up a time for the four of us to sit down. You know I like to have my wife sit in on these meetings?"

"Yes, sir, and thank you for your time." Micah shook the hand of the pastor, just as others were trying to make their way over to him.

"Anytime, Micah." He patted his shoulder, as he walked away, to speak with other parishioners.

~~~~~~~~~~~~~~~~~~~~

Sunday dinner was lively, as ever. Mother Salester was in rare form, telling her most humorous stories of old. She recalled her childhood memories and all the situations she and her friends found themselves in. Preston, Aaron, Anise, Desmond, and Kathleen laughed, until tears fell from their eyes, while listening to the matriarch of the family.

"Mother Salester, you are such a ham." Kathleen said. "I love when you share your past with us."

"We, all, do Mother." Preston chimed in.

"Babies, God gave us a history to share. It is how His word has been passed down. We are to repeat His goodness, babies. Never forget to rehearse the Lord's bountiful blessings with your children and convince them to share it with their children. This is how our legacy stays alive and gets its strength." Mother Salester turned to speak to Preston.

"I know God has shared something with you. Do not doubt it and do not be afraid. You are ready, son. He has given you everything you need to be a success and blessing. I pray God sees fit to allow me to live long enough to partake of the good thing He has prepared for you." Joyful tears flowed from her eyes, as she reached her arms out to her eldest grandson.

"What are you talking about, Mother?" Kathleen asked.

"That is between God and Preston. When he is in the position to know he hears God, he will shout it from the rooftops." Mother Salester winked, at Preston.

Everyone looked between Preston and Mother Salester, inquisitively; then shrugged their shoulders, letting the secret remain until one of them was ready to share it.

"I am ready for dessert, Mama." Aaron said, as he headed toward the kitchen. "What did you make, this week?"

"There is coconut cake, in the refrigerator, baby." Kathleen answered.

"I want cake, too, Grandma." David chirped.

"Of course, Grandma's baby wants cake. So, Grandma will get you some cake." Kathleen jumped up, grabbed David's hand and led him to the kitchen.

CHAPTER TWENTY-ONE

Dominion Counseling and Wellness Center was located in the center of town, in Portsmouth Virginia. Tamu Singletary smiled, every time she walked through the doors of her dream. She switched on the lights, pressed the code to turn off the alarm and looked around. She checked each office, to insure they were clean and ready for the business of the day. She inspected the supply room, along with each of the medicine cabinets.

After a quick perusal of the cafeteria area, then off to her office to check the messages from the weekend. With pen, in hand, she listened for any calls that demanded her immediate attention. There was an urgent plea from one of her newest clients. She had a particularly rough weekend and inquired about an earlier appointment time, this morning. She reached into the file drawer, pulled out her file and picked up the receiver to dial her number.

Tamu glanced up, just in time to see Mary Jane Hall walking toward her office. The two women waved a fleeting greeting, just before the patient answered the call.

"Good morning, Sonia. I just received your message and called right away. I am sorry to hear there was some stress over the weekend. I have a free slot, first thing, this morning. So, feel free to come in, as soon as you are ready." Tamu listened while Sonia gave a brief synopsis of the events of that had transpired, then concluded the call by penciling her name in the 8:30 am slot, for the day.

Tamu pushed back the purple leather office chair. She turned to take a look around the grounds, just outside of her window. She loved watching the ducks playing in the pond and listening to the birds chirping in the trees. Pride swelled up, within her, each time she thought about how blessed she felt with getting this piece of property to open the wellness center. She had been spying out the land, before she consulted with the real estate agent to put a bid on the building.

She walked out into the hall to bask in the sunlight which poured through the glass ceiling, filling the entire atrium. Tamu glanced toward Mary's office to see her pulling out the files for her clients of the day. She decided she would go in and chat with her, while the morning was still young. The two of them were, always, the first to arrive, which brought her delight. Another blessing, Tamu mused to herself, whenever she thought of her being able to hire Mary on as the Director of Nutrition at the Center.

Mary did an excellent job with the Million Pound entrants, as well the clients who walked through the doors looking for help with controlling diabetes or losing weight to lower their cholesterol or blood pressure. She graduated top of her class and came highly recommended by those she interned with, during her college years. There were programs, Mary had implemented, which were unprecedented in her field. Many of her colleagues called for consults and sent referrals for patients which were proving resistant to their regime.

Tamu knocked on the office door and waited for acknowledgement before entering in. "Good morning, Mary."

"Hello, Tamu. How was your weekend? Did you and Aaron do anything exciting?" Mary smiled, while peering through charts.

"The weekend was great. We spent Saturday, together. We went out to dinner, then to the beach. He spends Sundays with his family. This week, I did not go with him, I stayed home to catch up on some reading." Tamu took a seat, opposite Mary.

"You two have been an item for quite some time and the fire stills burns hot. I am hoping the same for Garrison and I. He is attentive and romantic, which is making it difficult for me, at times." Mary turned her attention to Tamu.

"Well, I think a lot of what keeps the embers aflame with Aaron and I, is the age difference. I am coming into my prime at the same time he is coming into his. There are many of my friends who gossip about us, calling me a cougar, and all." The two laughed.

"I say, do you, Tamu!" Again, they shared a giggle.

"Oh yes, I am doing me, alright. I don't care what those caddy broads have to say. We are happy and that is all that matters to us. His family is incredible, which bodes well if we decide to settle into marriage." Tamu paused, briefly. "Speaking of marriage, how are the plans coming for your upcoming nuptials?"

"It cannot happen soon enough, is what I have to say. We are interested in a destination wedding, however, we are uncertain of romantic locations, which are affordable for all who we would like to attend." Mary stated.

"Well, if you do not mind a bit of help, I may have something in mind." Tamu had an excited look on her face.

"I'm listening." Mary asserted.

"Well, Aaron and I have purchased a timeshare in Aruba. They have large villas which are located, directly, on the beachfront. There is a large sitting area, which will be perfect for an intimate indoor reception. It has French doors that lead out to a patio, with a walkway leading to the water." Tamu could barely contain herself.

"You have my attention." The glint, in Mary's eyes, was evident.

"The villas have several bedrooms and bathrooms, large eat-in-kitchens, which connect to the seating area, I mentioned earlier." She looked over at MJ. "Any of this interesting you?" She smiled.

"Are you kidding me?" Mary squealed. "Can we go next weekend?"

"Well, not that soon. However, I can look into something within the next sixty days, if that is not placing too much of a demand on your plans." Tamu queried.

"If you are serious and after you talk it over with Aaron, as we would be taking your slot for the year, I will speak with Garrison to see what he says." Mary raised her eyebrow.

"I will call Aaron, today, as soon as I have a free moment. You will have our answer before day's end." Tamu glanced over at the wall clock. "Well, let me get into my office. I am expecting a client, momentarily. Have a fantastic day, Mary." She rose from the chair and walked out of the office.

CHAPTER TWENTY-TWO

Several weeks passed since the mini meltdown Ariel experienced. Her spirit was still a little askew, but she felt like she was on the mend. She returned to work, the following week, met with concerned looks from the lawyers and their paralegals. Micah was her perpetual lunch date, as they took the time for prayer and bible reading. He felt it was necessary to help cleanse their hearts and minds of the sin.

The embarrassment that ensued her finding out that Preston knew of their fall was great. Yet, Micah assured her that he would never judge them, only pray and encourage them to stay focused on God and His plan for their lives.

Ariel recalled the conversation she and Micah had that Saturday morning, after Damaris left for home. He advised that Preston berated him for stepping outside of God's perfect plan for couples. Lust's conclusion was a sex act, whereas the marriage bed is undefiled because the couple used it to get to know one another, completely. Sex was a temporary release, where lovemaking is designed to cause the couple to draw closer to one another in spirit, mind and body.

Micah apologized to Ariel for allowing him self to lose sight of the big picture for their lives. He sought her forgiveness because he disrespected her and the role she plays, in his life. He would not let her take the onus for his part. He did assert that there was a conversation she needed to have with the Lord. He knew she had not prayed about the situation because of her silence and subsequent hiding.

He prayed for and with her, right over the phone. He thanked God for allowing them to realize their sin and trust His grace to be sufficient for their needs. They both accepted the blood covering for their sin and applied it to their lives and heart, again.

Ariel had hung up the phone, walked upstairs to her bedroom and into the master bathroom to run herself a bath. She undressed and stepped into the steaming water and immersed her entire body, before settling her head on the bath pillow. She let tears of relief and gratitude streamed down her face, while she soaked away the darkness that had surrounded her, for a week.

She prepared to meet with the girls, to choose bridesmaid dresses for MJ's wedding. They were to meet with a consultant, this afternoon, to decide on the appropriate fabric for a winter wedding in Aruba. Damaris, Ariel and Sela could, barely, contain themselves when MJ told them where they were to travel for the ceremony.

Ariel was able to get information for air travel and rental cars, through her connections with the travel agency used by Brookes and Brooks. After Tamu's villa idea fell through, due to booking issues, MJ contacted Lissy Lampe, in Aruba; the wedding coordinator at the Manchebo Beach Resort and Spa.

The honking of a car's horn alerted Ariel of the arrival of the girls to pick her up. She grabbed her purse and keys, as she rushed out of the house. After locking the door, she rushed off the porch and hopped into MJ's Toyota Avalon.

"Hello, everybody!" Ariel greeted.

"Hey girl." Damaris, MJ and Sela replied.

"How is that fine man of yours?" Sela asked.

"Micah is wonderful." Ariel said.

"Is there any chance we will run into him, this afternoon?" Sela continued.

"I doubt that, Sela. I cannot imagine why they would be anywhere near the bridal section of Nordstrom's." Ariel chuckled.

"Just checking." Sela replied

The other women shook their heads, letting their questions fall to the wayside.

"Anyway...MJ, have you decided on the colors, for the wedding? I am excited about going to Aruba, as it has always been one of my dream vacations." There was excitement, in Damaris' voice, as she spoke.

"Well, I was thinking of coral strapless dresses and linen pants and shirts for the fellas, in sand." MJ peered through the rearview mirror to see the response.

"I think it sounds fantastic." Ariel was the first to reply.

"Oh yes!" Sela agreed. "I look good in anything!"

"Men look especially handsome in light colored linen attire." Damaris added. "I believe you have chosen great combinations for a beach wedding."

"I still cannot believe this is happening. It has the ring of a fairy tale…secret crush in high school leads to marriage, when couple reunites years later." MJ stated. "I would never have imagined it being the story of my life!"

"Why not you? MJ, you deserve this. Shoot, we all do!" Damaris laughed.

"Speak for yourself, young lady. I am not the one to settle down and kick back with the same man for the rest of my life. Oh no!" Sela asserted. "You girls can have all of that. Leave me out of that fantasy."

"Well, you never know, Sela. You may find yourself some island man, in Aruba, and change that tune, altogether." MJ shot back.

Sela rolled her eyes and turned her head toward the window. "None of that for me; thank you."

"We will see you change your tune, one day. I am certain of it."Damaris concluded.

"You keep dreaming, baby girl. I will be sorry to disappoint you."

Everyone laughed as MJ pulled into a parking space at McArthur Center Mall, in Norfolk. They would be early for the appointment she had scheduled, with one of the consultants, at Nordstrom's, so they decided to swing by Smoothie Mania.

"Who is the consultant we will be working with, in Nordstrom's?" Damaris asked.

"Her name is Marshallan Monroe. She is, also, one of the buyers and comes highly recommended by one of the clients, in the Wellness Center." MJ started. "So, I gave her a call and was glad when she could squeeze us in, just before her trip to Paris."

"If she is that good, I will get her card for my wedding." Ariel said.

"Hey, is there something we should know?" Sela inquired.

"Nothing definitive, to talk about, at the moment. However, Micah and I do not see our selves with anyone else, and he is making plans for our future. We have had several discussions of marriage, over the years."

"Wouldn't it be a hoot, for the two of us to married within the same year?" MJ stated.

"I would be ecstatic, to say the least. Micah is holding off, so he will be financially stable. He is a stickler for plans...dotting every "I" and crossing every "T" as the old folks would say." Ariel sighed. "I just want to marry the man I love and allow the chips to fall where they may."

"There is nothing wrong with planning. Plus, the two of you are a perfect balance. God will bring it all into fruition, in His timing. I'm excited for and celebrating both you and MJ." Damaris encouraged.

"We will see. Right now, it's all about MJ!" Ariel added, as she finished her small strawberry-banana smoothie.

"Indeed." Damaris agreed, slurping the remnants of the Mango-Pineapple drink.

The friends pushed back their seats and headed toward the exit and the garbage. After tossing the emptied cups into the receptacle, they walked out, heading toward the entrance of Nordstrom's to locate Marshallan Monroe's office.

CHAPTER TWENTY-THREE

Marshallan Monroe sat behind her desk and crossed her long legs, at the ankle. She peered into her appointment book, taking note of what is next, for her day. She loved her job, as a buyer and consultant for Nordstrom's. All throughout college and her internships, she was excited about the prospect of doing what she loved and getting paid for it. There were few women who possessed the fashion acumen with which she has been blessed. She was a forward thinker, with a keen insight into what the fashion world would be looking for as the next craze.

When she received the call from Nordstrom's, after her internship with Bloomingdale's didn't produce a job, she was ecstatic. She called her mother, who proved to be her biggest fan and strongest force in pushing her forward into her dreams.

"Ma Dear" as Marshallan, affectionately, called her mom never allowed her to wallow in defeat. There were no obstacles with which she felt she could not overcome, as she could not quit. No room was made to back down from a challenge or cringe when things looked more difficult than first imagined. Setbacks were opportunities to prove that nothing could keep her from accomplishing her goals.

A smile crossed Marshallan's face as she thought how this particular mindset yielded her the fruits that others were incapable of enjoying. She did not take 'no' for an answer, from anyone. When she set her mind to a task, the end result benefitted her, sometimes at the expense of others. Survival of the fittest is an adage with which she governs her every day. She lives a life of little regret, which caused her to have a small circle of female friends.

Manicured hands reached for the phone, as it rang. Marshallan's secretary was calling to alert her of the arrival of her next appointment. She stood and smoothed her pencil skirt over her slender hips. After insuring the silk blouse fell, perfectly, over her ample breasts and every hair was in place she walked over to the office door, inviting the women in.

"Hello, ladies." Marshallan greeted. "Which one of you is the bride to be?"

"That would be me." MJ beamed, as she reached for the extended hand and shook.

"Let me congratulate you, on your upcoming nuptials. It is my pleasure to assist you with your choice of attire for your special day and the following days, if it is your wish." Marshallan looked at the other women. "Is this the bridal party?"

"Yes. This is Damaris Rhenay, Sela Brown and Ariel Jackson." MJ stepped aside, as each greeted Marshallan.

"Is there a maid or matron of honor, in the bunch?" Marshallon asked as she offered seats to the women and took her chair behind the desk.

"No distinction made between them." MJ stated.

"Okay, okay. Well, let's get started, shall we? Tell me your wardrobe dream for this special occasion." Marshallan flashed a dazzling white smile, in MJ's direction.

"Do you have any books or catalogs for me to look through?" MJ asked.

"No, dear, I do not work that way. I get sight of your vision by listening to you, and then I shop the world to find your dream. We are not trying to dress you like other brides and bride's maids. It is your unique day, therefore, a unique dress. Is that alright, with you?" Marshallon queried.

The friends looked at each other with impressed looks upon their faces. Marshallan was pleased with the expressions she witnessed. She never grew weary watching people's astonishment at her claims. She was not one for empty words, as she could produce on every claim.

"Of course, that is fine with me." MJ smiled.

"Great! Now, let's start, again." Marshallan sat back, folding her hands. "Tell me your dream."

MJ began to unfold the vision of her perfect wedding day and dress. She spoke, freely, about how she pictured the girls and the guys; the colors she thought would work on the white sandy beaches of Aruba. Marshallan listened, intently, as the scene was painted for her.

It wasn't until MJ had finished speaking, that Marshallan took out a pad and pencil. She quickly sketched out her version of what she had heard, while the women sat by, silently.

When she turned the pad to MJ, her jaw dropped and her eyes widened in astonishment. She was looking down at an exact replica of what she had seen in her dreams. "Marshallan, I do not know what to say. I am flabbergasted. You have a gift!" MJ exclaimed.

"My name is pronounced, Mar-shell-in."

"I apologize."

"It is an easy mistake. No hard feelings." Marshallan assured. "So, what do you think? Is that what I should be looking for, MJ?"

"It is exactly what I envisioned. Will you be able to find this dress and have it shipped here, within the month?" MJ asked.

Marshallan smiled. "If that is what you want, it can be here, within a couple of weeks."

"And the brides maids dresses?" Sela questioned.

"Ms. Brown, if Ms. Hall is completely satisfied with the sketches and is certain she is ready to commit, every dress will arrive within the same timeframe." Marshallan returned her gaze to MJ. "The decision is yours."

"If what you have drawn is what I will receive, I am fully ready." The excitement in MJ's voice was evident.

"Very well..." Marshallan stood, after pulling a tape measure out of the side drawer. "Let's get started. I need each of you to strip down to the bare essentials, so I can get measurements. If you are uncomfortable dressing and undressing in front of each other, we can do this one at a time. It is up to you." She waited.

CHAPTER TWENTY-FOUR

Since her early teenage years, Damaris has missed Thanksgivings on Stags Head Road in Towson, Maryland. She could remember the dinner being prepared by the kitchen staff, while she ran down the street to Ariel's house. She loved sitting around the kitchen table, while the matriarchs gossiped and cooked their own food.

The girls would giggle, as Ariel's grandmother would talk about the elderly women in the church and her mother would attempt to quell her wagging tongue. They loved to listen to Grandmother go on and on, as if her daughter was not compelling her to cease her chatter about the women of God.

Both girls loved to lick their fingers after wiping out the bowls once the pies and cakes were put into the oven. They would swing their feet, while their faces got sticky with the batter. Ariel's family welcomed Damaris as one of their own, so she had chores during the Thanksgiving prep time. She would wipe of the counters and table, while Ariel dried the dishes after the grown-ups finished washing them.

While dinner cooked at Ariel's house, the girls would run back to the Rhenay's and eat a light brunch, to tide them over until the meal was ready at the Jackson's.

This year was no exception. She longed for the comfort of a close family, during the holidays. The Rhenay's special moments were spent around a formal dining room table, where her parents sat on either end. Dinners were quiet, save the occasional clank of the utensils against the fine china. Talk was for the family room, after the meal had been completed.

So, when Preston invited her to his family's Thanksgiving celebration, she accepted, quickly. He had been sharing, with her, about the Sunday dinners and she secretly wanted to be asked to participate. Now was her opportunity to sit with a family that sounded like the Jacksons.

As she shared the great news with Ariel, she found out that Preston had invited her, as well. Micah would be there, as his usual custom to share holiday meals with the Lambert's, since he was a teenage boy. Damaris' heart was filled with gratitude that she would be sharing the holiday with her best friend and a man she has come to care for, deeply.

Over the past few weeks, she and Preston had spoken, daily. They shared several lunches and frequented many art galleries in the Chesapeake area. She hoped he would ask her to dinner or a movie, however, that hasn't happened, yet. Damaris remained hopeful, though.

As time has moved on, there has been a molten liquid seeping into Damaris' mind and spirit, of which she could not halt. It made its way into small crevices and minute corners. Its warmth could be felt in her very core and it emanated through her pores. Her soul was illuminated with its brilliance and it was evident to the casual observer. Her co-workers recognized it, yet could not pinpoint an origin. There was something different about her, was all that could be said.

Damaris lived with its effulgence, as a daily companion, since God had spoken to her in regard to one, Preston Lambert. She questioned the Lord about the blazing river that coursed through her. His answer was to allow it access and free reign. She was not to attempt to offset it or look to be loosed from it. This was His doing, thus she was not to be afraid. So, she has allowed it to course through her, knowing she would not be overwhelmed; even when the magnitude of it seemed to rise up in her chest and suffocate her.

The river was changing her for the better. She was peaceful and serene, most of the time. It seemed the river swelled in waves, as she and Preston spent more time together. Damaris wanted to label it, yet God would not permit her to do so. His Spirit compelled her to trust Him and the work He was doing, in and through her.

She was experiencing this tropical wave, as she prepared for Thanksgiving dinner with the Lambert's. Preston was coming by in a couple of hours and Damaris' spirit was being washed in the aqueous solution of which she could not define. She sat down on her white leather sofa, trying to quell the surge. She thought she felt faint, yet it wasn't quite the word to describe the feeling.

Damaris mouthed a 'thank you, God' when she realized the phone was on the couch, as it rang. She was certain she would not have been able to get up, at the moment. "Hello." She answered.

"Hello, Damaris." Preston replied. "Are you feeling alright? I sense something in your voice."

She should not be amazed, as this has been happening since he prayed for her on the morning of MJ's engagement dinner. However, it still caught her off guard. "Preston, I do not know how you do it. Every time there is something going on, you call and pick up on it, right away."

"Are you not feeling well?" Preston knew what Damaris was referring to, as he recognized the uncanny knack that he has developed for her. However, he could not put a lock on *what* was going on, just that something was.

"I would not say that I am not feeling well. I will say that I am experiencing something that is indiscernible. I would not call it an uncomfortable feeling, it is more unchartered, if that makes sense." She berated herself for not being able to identify and relay her emotions.

"Surprisingly, it does make sense. I have been experiencing something akin to that, if I can use your words; it is indiscernible." Preston spoke further. "It is as if there is a river running through my spirit. It is a spiritual thing, of that I am certain, however I cannot quite put a label on it."

"Exactly!" Damaris agreed, excitedly. "The river is permeating my entire being. There is no place that has not been affected by the flow. It is constantly moving into every..."

"...empty place that is within me." Preston completed.

"Yes."

"It is almost like this river is setting up residence in the sinews and marrow of my body." Preston continued.

"It's furnishing the dark places." Damaris spoke, as if in a trance.

"Places left open, intentionally, by God for this very purpose." Preston sensed a dawning, deep within his being. The light, which is the river, shone ever brighter.

As Damaris sat on the sofa, she sensed a discernment welling up with the fiery sea. The liquid brimmed out of her eyes and down her cheeks. She felt God, in the room, and she grasped the phone with two hands. She knew the Lord was speaking and she wanted to hear it, as Preston spoke.

"I love you, Damaris Rhenay." Preston's voice sounded like the wind over the ocean.

"I love you, Preston Lambert." Damaris breathed, in reply.

CHAPTER TWENTY-FIVE

Preston spent the entire Thanksgiving dinner, in quiet reflection. He interacted with everyone, watched the game with the fellas and helped with the dishes. However, his mind was flooded with the river of love which God has caused to spring forth for His daughter, Damaris Rhenay. He wondered why he had not been able to ascertain the emotion before now. He wondered how long had she been bathed in the tsunami, which she described.

The ride to his mother's house was spent in reverence to the Spirit of God which could still be felt, when he arrived to pick up Damaris. They shared a brief kiss, yet the embrace was filled with the river's fire. Damaris cried as Preston wiped her face with his handkerchief (which he assured her was clean). There was no embarrassment between them. There was no awkward moments shared. They, simply, were in love and it was as the Lord wished. Neither of them felt it necessary to expound on the revelation or attempt to make sense of its timing or origin.

Preston had taken her hand and they walked to his car, in silence. He opened the passenger door and stepped aside, giving

Damaris access. He shut it and made his way to the driver's side and took his seat. As he backed out of the driveway, he felt Damaris' hand upon his and he stroked it with his thumb. The love was palpable. It seemed to be an entity, in and of it self. It took a seat, in the hearts of the two riders and reached out invisible arms to bind them, together.

His family loved Damaris. Preston made the introductions and stepped aside to watch her interact with his mother and grandmother. His sister grabbed her around the shoulder and led her to the kitchen, asking questions as they went along. Mother Salester looked over at Preston and nodded, in approval.

"I told you trust that God knew what He was doing." Mother Salester called back, as she made her way to the kitchen with the other women.

Preston smiled. "You were right, again." He called back.

He could sense Damaris smile, as she listened, and he smiled all the more. He shook his head, in awe, at the workings of God. He raised his hands, in thanksgiving and adoration, right in the middle of the hall. The Lord had answered his prayers in a way that superseded his requests, just as His Word promised.

Now, as the day's festivities were nearing an end, Preston could hear Mother Salester invite Damaris to Sunday dinner. She assured her it would just be leftovers, but the communion would be great.

Damaris graciously accepted the offer and asked if there was something she could bring. Mother Salester raised her eyebrow, in question. "Can you cook, sweetie?"

"Yes, ma'am." Damaris, simply, replied.

"Well, surprise us." Mother Salester offered.

"I will do that." Damaris leaned down to kiss the cheek of the matriarch of the Lambert's family. Afterward, she made her rounds to everyone, hugging and kissing her goodbyes.

"I like this girl." Kathleen told her son, as he leaned in to hug and kiss his mother.

"I am glad. I believe she will be your daughter-in-law." He whispered in her ear.

Kathleen gasped, as she covered her mouth. Preston put his finger up to his lips to quiet her, as he saw the tears welling up in mother's eyes. She pulled him close, "Oh Preston," was all she could mutter.

"What is going on over there, between you two?" Anise questioned, looking inquisitively.

"It is between Mama and me." Preston asserted.

Anise looked over to Damaris, "Don't look at me. I have no idea what is happening. I am just a guest." She put her hands up, in defense.

After Preston picked up his nephew and twirled him around, he hugged Aaron, Micah and Desmond, then kissed Tamu, Ariel and Anise on the cheek. "See you guys, on Sunday." He yelled out, as he and Damaris walked out of the door.

As they drove, Preston began to open up. "Damaris, I want you to know that I have been seeking the Lord for a wife. He gave me an assurance that I would know her by the Spirit. I trust God, with my entire life, and I know He will never lead me astray. This love, is born of the Father, there is no denying that. We did not seek it out, between the two of us; yet, it is tangible. It is anointed and blessed." He turned to face her, as he came to a traffic light. "I am not asking you to marry me, yet I am not looking for a girlfriend to date. I am not a school boy on a quest to see how many women I can get to go out with me." Cars began to honk, as the light turned green.

Preston continued driving and speaking. "I do not want to frighten or overwhelm you, however I am certain God has spoken to you, as well."

"He has Preston. We are on the same page. We have, both, been given word by God as it relates to the two of us. I am not one to grieve the Holy Spirit with denials." She grabbed his free hand with both of her hands. "I am profoundly in love with you, Preston Lambert. It wasn't planned or fostered, it is of God. So, when God speaks to you about the timing, my answer will be yes."

Preston pulled over onto the side of the road and put the car in 'park.' He reached over and gently pulled Damaris to him. The look in his eyes caused her breath to catch, in her throat. It was so powerful and filled with such love, it washed over her. She closed her eyes, in anticipation, and she felt his mouth upon hers. His lips were hot and his tongue was like a branding iron, as it gently grazed across hers.

He was claiming his bride, in that very moment. She reached her hands around his neck and grasped the back of his head, as she welcomed the emblazoned kiss.

Damaris was melting into the mellifluous liquidity. She felt herself meld into Preston so much so there was no separation between the two souls. Their breathing was in sync, as the kiss deepened into a spiritual embrace.

Before she knew it, Damaris was on her knees and wrapping her arms around Preston welcoming him into her soul. His breath was that of a furnace, his hands were soldering irons. They seemed to burn her skin, as his tongue did her mouth, yet she wanted more.

He pulled her onto his lap; however, there was no physical sign of the intensity of their embrace. Preston, simply, wanted Damaris closer to him as he shared the love he was feeling for her spirit. The heat emanating from their bodies caused the windows to cloud over.

The kiss was languishing and sensual, yet lust did not overpower them. Tears fell onto Preston's cheeks, as Damaris cried, silently. She laid her head onto his shoulder, sinking more and more into an embrace which knit their spirits, together.

After a few minutes, Preston placed Damaris back in the passenger seat and lowered the windows to clear the air, in the car. He leaned back, closed his eyes and took a deep breath, before he put the car in 'drive' and pulled out onto the main road.

CHAPTER TWENTY-SIX

"Don't allow yourself to be worn down by the tactics of the enemy to wear you out. Stay focused on things of spiritual value, and keep your emotions in check. You can overcome by resisting this attack. Be energized by knowing that you have the victory and that no weapon formed against you will prosper. Stand strong. Be strong."

Micah replayed the message Preston had left for him, after that fateful day of his transgression. His friend did not want him to get down on himself and get stuck in condemnation and never experience the love of God's conviction. He listened to it, often, to help remind him to keep plodding forward.

He walked through his house, in his pajama pants and tee shirt, as instrumental jazz played on the stereo. He sat down, in his favorite chair and put his feet up on the ottoman. He leaned his head back against the high back of the chair and closed his eyes. He counted himself blessed, as he prayed to God, asking for His guidance for the next phase of his life.

He had his meeting with the Pastor, on yesterday, and was pleased with the outcome.

He felt confident in his decision to marry Ariel and realized that he was leaving the door open for the enemy by putting it off. He contemplated his approach and how he would pop the question. He wondered if putting the ring in a Christmas present would be romantic.

He picked up the phone to place a call to Ariel. He listened and waited for her to pick up. "Hello." Ariel answered.

"Hey baby. What are you doing?"

"Micah, I am glad you called. We need to talk." There was a note of sadness in Ariel's voice.

"Sure. Sure. Do you want to discuss it over the phone? Or would you prefer I come over?"

"I'm pregnant."

The silence that followed caused Ariel's heart to sink, into her stomach. She would not allow her mind to run rampant. There were thoughts attempting to invade and crush the peace she had been pursuing, after the incident in her driveway. She cringed every time she thought of the lascivious manner in which she had behaved that night. The shame lurked around her, like a stalker, seeking entrance. It wanted to possess her, weighing her down with its talons.

Tears ran down her cheeks, as she willed Micah to speak up and quell the furious onslaught. "Please say something...anything." Ariel breathed out.

Micah released the breath he had been holding, in a long ragged sigh. "I'm sorry, Ariel."

"Sorry does not begin to describe the torment of despair I have been enduring since reading the test strip. What are we going to do, Micah?" Ariel cried, freely.

"Baby, everything will work out. God knew this was going to happen and there have been provisions, in place, before the foundation of the world. We have confessed our fault and we have been forgiven. The first step is for us to get married. I will not have a child of man born into the world, out of wedlock." Micah scrambled for the right words to say to Ariel. His heart raced and his head began to pound at the enormity of what the two of them faced.

"Are you just saying that because I am pregnant, Micah? The last thing I want is a shotgun wedding." Ariel sniffed.

"Baby, I was calling you to invite you over for this very reason. I was going to propose, this evening. Aside from my botched proposal plans, this is exactly what I want. Is it what you want, Ariel?" Micah questioned, realizing he had yet to ask for her answer.

"I have been waiting for you to propose to me, for months. Of course, I want to marry you, Micah Alexander." Ariel giggled, feeling relieved.

"Well then, it is settled. Ariel Jackson will soon become Ariel Alexander." Micah smiled. "That has a nice ring to it, wouldn't you say?"

"Yes, it does." Ariel agreed.

"Perfect." Micah stated.

"I have not gone to the obstetrician, yet. However, by my calculations, I am nearly five months along. With that in mind, I have missed critical appointments and I hope everything is alright." Ariel offered.

"Did you not miss your cycle?" Micah asked.

"My cycle has never been regular. I had been feeling queasy, but I attributed that to the constant punishing of myself. The only thing that assuaged the nausea was for me to eat...thus an explanation for the weight gain I have experienced."

Micah had noticed a change in Ariel's appearance. However that is a subject that men shied away. "Have you contacted a doctor, already?"

"Yes. I have an appointment next week. Would you like to come along?"

"Of course, just let me know the date and time. We can leave work, together, if that is alright with you."

"That will be fine, Micah. The check up is scheduled for Wednesday, mid-morning." Ariel was smiling now. She knew there was much to account for and own up to, yet she was ready to face it, as long as Micah was there to support her.

"Let me get dressed, and I will be right over." Micah stated, as he rose from his seat.

"Okay, Micah. I will see you when you get here. I have some phone calls I need to make, before you arrive." Ariel walked over to the kitchen and opened the refrigerator, to get a bottle of water. She rubbed her belly and immediately felt ripples that resembled the nervous feeling associated with fluttering butterflies.

"Well, hello there." She spoke aloud to her stomach, as she returned to the sofa.

CHAPTER TWENTY-SEVEN

A bolt of lightning raced toward the ground, just as a clap of thunder burst forth through the heavens. The heavy downpour cleared everything in its path, leaving in its wake pristine streets, sidewalks and driveways. The rain beat against the window pane of Damaris' bedroom, appearing as one solid sheet of water. The winds raged, as the unusual thunderstorm cleared the atmosphere. The temperatures had been unseasonably mild, as winter prepared to make its exit.

Damaris had been sprawled out, on her bed, peering into her closet wondering what she would pack for the trip to Aruba. Garrison and MJ's wedding was just a week away and everyone was scheduled to leave Virginia, in a couple of days. She needed to get something into her suitcase, soon, or she would begin to feel out-of-sorts with the looming deadline fast approaching.

With a sigh, she turned away from the closet and the empty suitcase sitting nearby. So much had transpired since Thanksgiving. She and Preston were an item; a bona fide couple. The two of them chose to alert their families during the Christmas holidays. His family were overjoyed, especially Mother Salester. It was as if God had spoken to her about the two of them before they were certain. It warmed her heart to be welcomed as one of the Lambert's, without missing a step. Her parents, on the other hand, were less enthusiastic.

As Damaris and Preston drove into the neighborhood of Riverwalk, in Chesapeake, she could feel her pulse quicken. She had spoken to her parents about Preston, once after Thanksgiving. She was concerned that they would not be as hospitable as the Lambert's had been to her.

"It will be fine, Damaris." Preston assured, as he placed his hand upon hers. His voice had a way of calming and exciting her, depending on the circumstance. At this moment, she could feel her heart return to its normal rhythm.

She smiled and grabbed his hand with her own. "If you say so, it shall be so."

"By the power given to me, as a child of the Most High God, I can decree a thing and it will come to pass." Preston's voice resonated with authority.

It gave Damaris goose bumps whenever Preston stood firm on his position as God's son. There was little, if any, doubt in his voice. He commands situations and circumstances to come in line with the will of God and God supports His word, as it is spoken out of Preston's mouth. He is a man of strong and resolute faith, who is certain of his station with his Lord.

Damaris could feel her body temperature rise, as she watched his mouth move and the power of his words filled the atmosphere. "You say that, baby!"

Preston smiled. He squeezed Damaris' hand, as he made the left turn onto Marina Reach off of Pepperwood Court. He signaled as he cornered Bottom Quay and made his way to the home of the Rhenays.

He pulled the Lexus into the driveway and turned the car off. He leaned toward Damaris, breathing softly. The scent from his cologne was intoxicating. She tasted the cinnamon Altoid as he brushed his tongue across hers. She closed her mouth around his bottom lip, gently pulling as he moved away.

Another loud clap of thunder shook her from the memory of that kiss and the subsequent cordial dinner she and Preston shared with her parents. He had been right, all went well that evening. Her parents embarrassed her with tales of her youth and the recanting of the drama-filled summer after their move from Maryland to Virginia. Preston laughed at the theatrical reenactment of the day of the move, by her mother, Sylvia.

Damaris smiled. Rainy days made her long for Preston's company. His presence, for her, was like a fire on a cold winter's night. He wrapped her in the warmth of his love and she was home. She prayed, fervently, that he felt like a ship docked after a long journey, whenever he was around her. She wanted to call him, however she knew there was work to be done. So, she resisted the urge to laze across the bed listening to the sexy voice of Preston Lambert.

She jumped up from the bed, suddenly realizing what she was going to pack into the suitcase. Perhaps she was being fueled by the thought of being able to play after her work was finished. Although there were no plans made, no evening expired without contact being made. Damaris wondered what Preston was doing, at this very moment. The bond they shared was intense and powerful. They had to take special care not to cross the line, so they made a pact never to spend time with each other in their private quarters. The two of them went even further and chose not to speak with each other, while lying in their respective beds.

Ariel and Micah's situation had been a rude awakening, for Preston and Damaris. Neither of them judged their friends for their moment of weakness, yet it strengthened their resolve to not break the oath they had taken. It was a difficult task, but they have been able to manage, thus far.

Damaris decided to call Ariel. She reached for the receiver and pushed the speed dial number. She waited while the phone rang.

"Hello." Ariel answered, sounding out of breath.

"Girl, what were you doing running up and down the stairs?" Damaris asked.

"This growing uterus has crowded into every nook and cranny of my abdomen. These twins are breaking a sister down, in the area of lung capacity." Ariel sat down. "Thank God Marshallan had the forethought to locate an alteration shop, near the resort, that will be able to do last minute adjustments."

"Marshallan Monroe is gifted and well connected. Whatever MJ paid was worth every penny." Damaris spread out across her bed, looking up at the ceiling. "So, Momma, how are you feeling besides being out of breath?"

"I am doing, as well as can be expected. I fight back tears thinking of how things could have been. It still bothers me that everything was done in reverse. I should have been married, prior to conceiving children. I wanted a very public wedding. My decisions made for an "intimate" ceremony in the pastor's office." Ariel continued, "And even though Micah assures me that he intended to marry prior to hearing the news of the pregnancy, I still have a nagging notion that I will never really know if that is the truth." She sighed.

"I guess I can understand your point." Damaris offered.

"Thank God I did not begin to show until after the ceremony. I do not know why that gives me a bit of comfort, but it does. At this point, I will take every bit of comfort I can get." Ariel laughed.

"It seems like you just shot out there, Ariel. It was like, one minute there was a little pouch and the next day you were toting around a beach ball under your shirt."

"Tell me about it. I, literally, had nothing to wear. What a blessing it has been that Micah was able to obtain a consult with Marshallan. With her help, Micah has been able to keep me very stylish in my Juicy Coutre and Michael Stars maternity clothes. She was even able to get me some beautiful dresses, by Olian and Chiarakruza, for Aruba." Ariel smiled.

"Your husband loves you." Damaris commented.

"I do not doubt that. He spends more time in Nordstrom's than I do." The two friends laughed. "Have you finished your packing, Damaris?"

"I am very close to being finished. I could not concentrate to pack, at first, because I could not keep my mind off Preston. I was listening to the storm and I wanted to feel him near me." Damaris sighed.

"Girl, you got it bad." Ariel joked.

"I do. I am profoundly in love with a man I have known less than year. Yet, I feel like I have known him all of my life. It is as if we were always a part of one another. Does that make sense?" Damaris questioned.

"You guys share a kindred spirit connection. I must admit, I wish Micah and I was in sync like that. Sometimes, I feel like there is some sort of disconnect between us." Sadness could be heard in Ariel's voice.

"What do you mean?"

"Don't get me wrong, we love each other. It feels like something is off, in the way we physically express that love; like there is a missing ingredient that causes me to wonder." Ariel stammered, "It's – it's like our puzzle pieces are forced matches, so the final picture is slightly askew."

"Are you referring to your sex life?" Damaris sounded concerned.

"Yes. It has never really taken off, like I'd hoped. The first time, quick...very quick and the subsequent moments we have shared were lackluster. Now that my belly has enlarged, it's awkward and frustrating." Ariel felt tears welling up. "I pray the reason is because of the pregnancy."

"You guys have a lot on your plates, at the moment. The marriage started off where others reach after a couple of years of getting to know one another. Give it time, sweetie." Damaris comforted.

"I hope you are right, Damaris. I would hate for Micah to get disenchanted with our sex life and look for spark elsewhere."

"You think Micah is cheating on you?" Damaris inquired.

"I would never accuse, without proof. I cannot be sure due to my lack of experience, but he is even less inspired to correct the issue than he once was. In the very beginning, we would try different things in an attempt to create a fire. Now, it's …" Ariel began to cry.

"I'm sorry, sweetie. Let's say it is the stressor of becoming a husband and father, so quickly. Do not upset yourself with thoughts of another woman. You need to give Nasarra and Nasir a comfy, stress-free environment in which to thrive." Damaris was concerned. "Is there something, else?"

Fresh tears flowed down Ariel's face. "I didn't want to talk about this before MJ's wedding, but, the sonogram indicated that something could be wrong with Nasarra. There is an abnormal growth in her brain."

"Oh my goodness, Ariel!" Damaris exclaimed.

"The perinatologist advised that we not get worked up, just yet. Another ultrasound is scheduled when we return from Aruba. She will measure the mass to determine if it is larger, then we will take it from there."

"It is so much to have to deal with, Ariel." Damaris spoke, as she wiped the tears from her face.

"No more than I can bear, right?" Ariel laughed.

"That is right."

"So, at the moment, I refuse to give in to the despair that seeks to wreck my soul. I will rejoice and be glad in every day God gives to me. I am going to have a fantastic time, in Aruba." Ariel spoke with false bravado.

"I will be praying for you, Micah and Nasarra. I know God's plans are sovereign and He is at work in the midst of your circumstance. He will reward your faith, sweetie." Damaris said.

"He already has. I have my moments, but for the most part, I have rolled this care over onto the Lord. I am staying focused on my marriage and the fact that I have two beautiful babies growing inside of me." Ariel was speaking to convince her friend. "Do not fret, Damaris. We serve an awesome God."

"Oh yes, we do! He is concerned with every aspect of our lives, so much so that He ordained good to come out of all things. It is not our place to determine what is good. We are to remained focused on the truth of all matters; God is good." Damaris was beginning to feel better. "God is the Creator of every living thing. He knows our downfalls and our uprisings. We are never lost from His sight. We are engraved on the palms of both of His hands – never to be snatched out."

"We are the head and not the tail. We are above and not beneath. We are blessed in the city and in the country; coming in and going out. Whenever the enemy comes in like a flood, the Lord raises a standard against him. We are to resist the devil, in order for him to flee. We are not to succumb to the wiles of the enemy as he attempts to trick us into following him down the road of despair." The two friends were encouraging one another.

"God will keep our minds, in perfect peace, as we keep our minds stayed on Him.

We are to trust in the Lord, with all of our hearts, and lean not to our own understanding. In all of our ways we are to acknowledge Him and He will direct our paths." Damaris continued.

"That is right, my friend. As we encourage one another and exhort each other in our most holy faith, God will succor us and keep us safe. My babies are in His care. Even in the womb, while their parts were yet unformed, God knew them. He knows them, still. They are safe." Ariel spoke.

"Yes, and no matter what facts present themselves, God's truth prevails...by His stripes, we were healed." Damaris smiled. "So, as little Miss Nasarra is under construction by the Master Potter, she is being formed and fashioned, in His likeness. She will live and not die..." Damaris started.

"...and declare the goodness of the Lord, in the land of the living." Ariel finished.

~~~~~~~~~~~~~~~~~~~~~~~

The flicker of the candlelight danced on the wall of the hotel room. Soft jazz played in the background, mingling with the sound of water running from the bathroom. Light giggles filled the air, as the man grabbed the woman around the waist. He did not want her to leave the bed. He pulled her on top of him, as his hands caressed the silky, smooth skin of her back.

"Leaving so soon?" The man questioned, as he planted soft kisses on the woman's shoulders and neck.

"Stop it." She giggled, again.

"I want more of you." He whispered, in her ear, as he nibbled gently.

"You have had all you are going to get, tonight." The woman swatted his hands away, as she arose from the bed, once more.

"But, I will be leaving, tomorrow to go to Aruba for my friend's wedding. Can't I have a little extra, for the road?" The man put his hands together, in a pleading fashion.

"I know you do." She stated.

"Why do you get to decide?" He asked, pouting like a petulant child.

"If I don't decide, then your wife will not see you until the morning. You may miss your plan trying to explain to her why you were out, all night." Marshallan waltzed her slender frame out of the room, closing the bathroom door behind her.

Micah placed the pillow over his face, muffling the scream, as he lay back onto the bed.

"You are right." He said, finally.

"I am, always, right." Marshallan called from the bathroom.

Micah could hear the splashing of the water and moaned, loudly. He arose from the bed, dressed and quietly walked out of the room.

CHAPTER TWENTY-EIGHT

Preston held Damaris' hand as they walked along the alabaster beach of Aruba's Caribbean waters. The moonlight shone, brightly off the shore, creating shadows along the shore. The few people, on the beach, were coupled off sharing in the splendor of the night. The stillness of the air, the soft lapping of the water and the muffled whispers created an ambiance that could not have been staged.

The intimacy and romance lingered on, from Garrison and MJ's wedding, which was held just a few hours before. Preston thought of the moment he would gaze into Damaris' eyes, as she walked down the aisle toward him, on their wedding day.

Ariel smiled, as they walked further along the beach. Preston asked, "What is putting that smile on your beautiful face?"

"I am thinking about your crazy friend, Garrison, singing Rick James', Mary Jane to MJ at the reception." She laughed out loud.

"MJ looked so embarrassed, as he belted out 'Come here, baby. Mary I love you." Preston joined in with the laughter.

"Oh, and when the DJ put the record on…" Damaris bent over, laughing.

"He just got louder! 'I'm in love with Mary Jane. She's my main thing. She makes me feel alright. She makes my heart sing.' We all hollered."

"Then, Sela gets into it, dancing around like she was one of the Mary Jane girls." Damaris was holding her stomach. "MJ couldn't help but smile, at his gesture."

"She reeled him in, though. When he got to the part where it says, 'Do you love me, Mary Jane?' She grabbed his face, mouthed 'Yes' then kissed him, passionately." Preston turned to Damaris. "Like this."

He wrapped his arms around her, pulling her tightly, to himself. Preston's mouth was warm and inviting. Damaris closed her eyes, allowing the kiss overtake her senses. She reached up to grab the nape of his neck, as she pressed her body, closer.

"Get a room, you two. Get a room!" Sela's voice broke through the moment.

Preston stepped back, without breaking the embrace. He looked down into Damaris' eyes and his expression spoke volumes. "There will be plenty of time…" He began before Sela caught up to them.

"You two holy rollers better cut that out. You know saved people get pregnant the first time they fornicate." Sela laughed.

"Sela, that is not something you need to be joking about, and you know it." Damaris reprimanded.

"It's just comedy."

"I don't think it is funny. It is in poor taste. You should not speak idly about matters that deal with your friends." Damaris continued.

"Alright. Alright." Sela conceded. "I will not make light of Ariel's condition or the circumstances that led up to it."

"Good. She needs our support, not ridicule."

"I said, 'alright.' Goodness." Sela said.

Preston was shaking his head, with a smile on his face. "You are going to take some getting used to, Sela."

"Yes, sir. You got that right. If you are going to be with my girl, you got to deal with me." Sela displayed a mock frown. "Don't mess with her. She is a treasure."

"Of this I am certain." Preston asserted.

"Anyway, what are you guys doing up, this late?" Sela asked.

"We are just spending some time, together, before we say goodnight." Damaris answered.

"You sure you wanna say goodnight? That kiss, I witnessed, looked like something, else." Sela raised her eyebrows at her friend.

"Sela, stop it." Damaris blushed. "We could ask you the same question...what are you doing out here, at this hour, alone?"

"Girl, I am looking for a party or club."

"On the beach?"

"Well, uh..." Sela stammered.

"Is that Jeremiah I see walking toward us?" Preston squinted in the darkness.

"Where?" Sela asked, a bit excitedly.

"What is that about?" Damaris looked over at her friend.

"Girl, don't meddle in grown folks business." Sela responded, as she trotted off toward Jeremiah.

Damaris and Preston shook their heads, as they watched their friends head in the opposite direction.

"There is something to be said about this island air and weddings." Preston said, as he took Damaris' hand.

"It is intoxicating." Damaris replied, as they continued on their way, in silence.

~~~~~~~~~~~~~~~~~~~~~~~~~~

Ariel lay, in bed, next to Micah wondering what she could do to get him to touch her. There was no medical reason for their abstinence. She turned toward him and put her arm across his torso. "Micah, what is the matter?"

"There is nothing the matter, Ariel. I am just concerned about the babies, Nasarra in particular. I do not want to do anything that may jeopardize the pregnancy." Micah replied.

"The doctor hasn't put any restrictions on our sex lives…." Ariel started.

"...I just don't feel comfortable." Micah interrupted.

Ariel pushed her disappointed aside in order to change the subject. "Well, have you thought anymore about the option to save the children's cord blood?"

"Are you kidding me?" Micah sat up, in bed. "You sound like you are planning on something going wrong, Ariel."

"That is not it, at all, Micah. We need to be proactive. God forbid, we find out that the growth on Nasarra's brain is a tumor. If we do not capture the cord blood, at the time of delivery, it will be too late." Ariel pleaded.

"Listen, I do not want to hear you speak cancer on our child. Do you hear me?" Micah demanded.

"I do hear you, Micah. However, let me say this to you. I am going to weigh every option and explore every avenue, necessary, to help insure Nasarra has the best chance. You can bury your head, in the sand, if you want. I will not do it." Ariel retorted.

"You are going to listen to Sela tell you what to do, like you cannot think for yourself?" Micah spit out.

"I have my own mind, Micah Alexander. These children belong to the both of us and we need to make sound, rational decisions that will be beneficial to them."

"You know what? Now is not the time to be talking about this, in the first place. We are on this beautiful island, Ariel. Let's table this conversation until we return home. Can we agree to do that?" Micah pleaded.

With a sigh, Ariel consented. Micah was right, now was not the time to discuss a matter of such grave importance. She recalled how uncomfortable she was when Sela first brought up the proactive actions people are taking to save the lives of their children.

Ariel had been reluctant, at first, to discuss the issue with Sela. There were times when she could be very insensitive. However, she knew her stuff when it came to her field of expertise. As the Clinical Research Coordinator, at Medical College of Virginia Hospital and a degree in Medical Technology, there was no denying the facts. Damaris convinced her it would be best to get piece of mind, prior to the trip, so she conceded.

The subject was broached, with Micah, casually over dinner, just before the trip to

Aruba. He did not want to entertain the idea of making plans for a medical emergency. He was not against preventative medicine; he would not give ear to the argument of gathering cord blood, just in case something went awry with the children.

Sela had given her bullet point to address during the conversation; it is like a rainy day savings fund; it is like buying an insurance policy and many others. He never denied that the premise was a good one; he couldn't bring himself to call his unborn child sick. His mind was focused on it being a bad omen and he would not do that to his child.

Ariel was frustrated with his bullheadedness on the subject. She was not going to allow Micah's superstitions keep her from doing what she felt was best, in this instance. Sure, it cost to have the cord blood cryogenically stored at the blood bank; but she would shoulder the responsibility, if needed.

"Micah, are you not attracted to me because I am fat?" Ariel asked.

"Where is this coming from? Baby, you are not fat. You are pregnant, with twins. You are beautiful." Micah answered.

Ariel leaned over Micah's shoulder, wrapping her arms around him. "Then show me, baby." She moved to kiss him, however he moved away.

"It is late, Ariel. Let's get some sleep. We have the rest of the week for me to show you."

Micah lay back on the bed and closed his eyes, while Ariel slid under the covers and wept.

~~~~~~~~~~~~~~~~~~~~~~~~~~~~~~~~~

MJ looked over to the tub and smiled. Garrison was waiting for her to join him, in the warm bubbles. He looked delicious. She had been waiting for this moment, since high school. The anticipation mounted, further, during the past few months; and now, the time had come. She would get her, first full taste of this beautiful man; her man; her husband.

She imagined she would feel self conscious standing naked, in front of Garrison. However, there was no anxiety or concern, as she walked over to the tub and took his waiting hand, while slipping into the tub. He pulled her onto his lap and her heart began to race, in anticipation. She did not want the moment to pass by, too quickly.

MJ pressed her body and her lips against Garrison's. His breath was hot, as he caressed her back and hips, then her legs. He kissed her neck and shoulders, as she leaned her body backward. Her mind reeled, as the passion became dizzying. The thought of taking it slow, was washed away, in an instant.

CHAPTER TWENTY-NINE

The week, in Aruba, was swiftly coming to an end and Damaris was looking melancholy.

"What is the matter, Damaris?" Preston asked, as they sat waiting for their lunch to arrive.

"I have enjoyed our time, here, in Aruba. I know we have to get back to our lives, but I don't want it to end." She took Preston's hand.

"I know what you mean."

"I imagine I will need a diversion to get my mind off of the impending flight back, tomorrow."

"I can bore you with menial chit chat about the weather, here in Aruba." Preston offered.

"Please, please bore me." Damaris said.

Preston proceeded to inform Damaris that Aruba experiencing a year-round summer, with a cool breeze, compliment of the trade winds. In the summer, the temperatures fluctuate between varying degrees in the eighties. There is very little rain, without the fear of drought.

During the winter months, Aruba is a paradise for windsurfers due to the prevailing trade winds. Preston educated Damaris stating the winds blow predominately from the northeast in the Northern Hemisphere and from the southeast in the Southern Hemisphere, thus causing them to strengthen during the winter.

Preston delved into history. The trade winds have been used by captains of sailing ships to cross the world's oceans for years. These winds enabled European expansion into the Americas and trade routes to become established across the Atlantic and Pacific Oceans. In meteorology, the trade winds act as the steering flow for tropical storms that form over the Atlantic, Pacific and South Indian Oceans and make landfall in North America.

"Aruba escapes the brunt of hurricanes and other tropical depressions, as the trade winds steer the storms away from the island." Preston added. "And the shallow cumulous clouds are capped from becoming taller, causing less rain."

"I love the fact that you know all of that." Damaris encouraged.

"I am a veritable wikipedia." Preston laughed.

"It is refreshing to know that I will never be bored with your conversation."

"I will, forever, be at your service, madam." Preston stated with an exaggerated waving of his hand.

"Forever?" Damaris grew serious.

"For as long as you will have me, sweet Damaris." Preston answered.

"As long as I will have you," Damaris repeated. "I look forward to having you."

"I dream about that moment." Preston's eyes grew dark and his voice was just above a whisper. He arose from his seat and came around the table to kneel in front of Damaris.

Tears welled up in her eyes as she realized the impact of this moment. Her heart beat erratically in her chest. Her breaths were labored.

"I cannot spend another moment without knowing that I have secured my future, with you. I pray you find me as the dock for your ship, Damaris Rhenay. My life is not my own and I am inspired by God in knowing you are my good thing. I have been searching, my whole life, for you." Preston reached into the pocket of his linen pants and pulled out a small velvet box.

Damaris gasped, as he opened the box to reveal a heart-shaped, colorless diamond ring. "Preston!"

The restaurant patrons looked on, as the couple shared a public, yet intimate moment.

"My breaths come easy, in your presence. I need you, in my life and hope you feel the same." Preston took the ring out of the box, waiting to place it on Damaris' finger. "Will you be my wife?" There were tears in his eyes.

Damaris offered her hand to Preston, "Yes! Yes, I will marry you." She squealed and hugged his neck.

The onlookers shouted their approval, as the couple kissed to consummate the engagement.

"When did you find time to get this ring, Preston?" Damaris asked, as she admired the sparkle of the three carat ring.

"Do you like it? Is it too much?" Preston inquired.

"Are you kidding me? I am going to the envy of every woman I know. I LOVE this ring." She squealed.

"A man finds ways to impress his lady and do it with an air of mystery."

"Enough said. I will not ask or concern myself with its origin. I will just enjoy it and the fact that I am going to be the wife of Preston Lambert. You are the man of my dreams, incarnate. I believe God has fashioned me to compliment you and for that I am grateful."

They kissed, again, and the restaurant exploded with applause. The waitress walked over to the table with plate with two cannolis. "Compliments of Chef Giorgio, to celebrate your engagement."

"Thank you." Preston and Damaris replied, in unison.

~~~~~~~~~~~~~~~~~~~

"The good book tells us it is better to marry than to burn." Sela said. "So, it is best that you two hot tamales tie the knot, so you can quench that fire." She laughed.

Damaris, MJ, Sela and Ariel sat in a shaded area of DePalm Island's water park,

Blue Parrotfish, while the men went off to locate beverages for the group. They were spending the late afternoon, on an outing for the entire wedding party. Everyone was scheduled to fly back to the states, except for the married couple. They were extending their stay, three days, in order to enjoy the quiet of the island.

"Girl, you are too much." MJ stated. "There should be fire between couples."

"Of course you would say that, Mrs. Newlywed. Let's see if you are still spouting the same words, this time next year." Sela scoffed.

"Not everyone allows their relationship to remain in a state of smoldering embers or snuffed out flames." Ariel added.

"Look at Ariel and Micah." Sela pointed. "Case and point; they haven't been married but a few months. Do they look like the Olympic torch? Are they still aflame?"

Ariel looked embarrassed. "You cannot use us as an example. The circumstances are very different, in our case."

"All I know, I don't see the fiery passion lingering around the two of you. I cannot remember ever seeing it, now that I think about it."

"Will you lighten up, Sela?" Damaris pleaded.

"Yeah, stop picking on Ariel. She needs our support and encouragement. She does not need us to highlight what can be better, in her life." MJ added.

"I am not picking on her." Sela defended herself.

"It's okay, girls. She is telling the truth and sometimes the truth hurts. Micah and I do not have that type of relationship." Ariel spoke.

"You cannot compare your relationship to anything or anyone. It just breeds dissatisfaction which is dangerous, in any relationship." Damaris said.

"I try not to compare, but when I look at the two of you and your relationships..."Ariel started.

"Here you go!" Micah interrupted as the men joined them.

Preston sat next to Damaris, Garrison next to MJ, Sela moved over to accommodate Jeremiah, leaving an empty place next to Ariel for Micah.

"Have you been showing off that ring of yours?" Garrison asked Damaris.

"The ring shows itself off!"Sela offered.

"Preston, you have outdone yourself with that piece of jewelry." Jeremiah added.

"I thank God Aruba has much to offer by way of fine jewelry." Preston said.

Damaris leaned in to kiss her fiancé. "I love it, sweetie."

"That's all that matters, to me." Preston returned the kiss.

Everyone finished their drinks and placed the cups in the nearby trash receptacle. Then they decided to head toward one of the park's breathtaking water slides.

"The thought of seeing you wet, MJ, is bringing back tantalizing memories." Garrison whispered.

"Well, I better sit, directly, in front of you to save you some embarrassment." MJ whispered, in return.

The friends enjoyed all that the water park had to offer, before showering and heading back to the hotel to change into their evening clothes. There was not much time before the boat would be sailing for the Fantasy Dinner and Dance Cruise.

As they arrived in the lobby to await transportation to the dock, Micah felt compelled to show his wife more attention, while around their friends. He did not want anyone to get the impression that there was trouble in paradise. He could not take his mind off of Marshallan and the things she would do to him, yet he did not want to rock the boat, on the home front.

Micah took Ariel's hand as they made their way to the transportation van. She looked into his eyes and smiled. "I love you, Micah."

"I love you, too, baby." Micah replied, being careful not to call a name, for fear of saying the wrong one. He remembered how Marshallan scolded him, the first time he called her Ariel.

He helped her into the van, and then jumped in behind her. The rest of the party, filed in and the van departed the hotel.

CHAPTER THIRTY

Kathleen concluded her lecture for the students who attended Norfolk State University. She allotted time for a question and answer session, as they readied themselves for the upcoming exam. She noticed a distinguished older man take a seat in the back room. At first, she did not think too much about it, as people were free to audit her class.

After the students filed out of the auditorium, she took note that the guest had not left with the others. She squinted, in an attempt to get a better look, however, the lighting was dim in that part of the room.

"Excuse me." Kathleen called out. "Is there something I with which I can assist you?"

The gentleman smiled. "Yes, ma'am there is." His voice was full, as it echoed throughout the hall.

Kathleen was taken aback by the affect his voice had on her. It was strange, yet familiar and a bit unnerving. "What can I do for you?"

"My name is Okency McIntyre." He answered, as he rose from his seat.

"Alright, Mr. McIntyre..." Kathleen began.

"Please, you can call me Okency." He replied.

"Okency, then. How may I help you?" If she were in a seat she would be fidgeting, Kathleen thought, as he walked toward her.

Okency McIntyre was a man of medium stature, standing just over five feet, ten inches. His skin tone was deep and rich with a few fine lines, accenting his caramel colored eyes. His nails were well manicured. His graying hair was cut close to his head. His teeth were even and very clean.

"Well, Mrs. Lambert, I have been observing you and your class for a few months. Today, is the first time I have made myself known to you." Okency reached for hand, in an offer to shake.

Kathleen took the proffered hand. "I am flattered."

Okency smiled at the confused expression which crossed Kathleen's face. "I am a fellow professor, here at the University. I teach one of the two military history courses, they offer."

"Pleased to make your acquaintance, Okency." Kathleen offered.

"The honor is all mine, Mrs. Lambert." Okency corrected.

"Feel free to call me Kathleen."

"Kathleen."

"I note a hint of an accent, are you from the islands."

"I am from the island of Haiti. You have a keen ear, Kathleen." Okency smiled.

"Tell me, to what do I owe this visit?" Kathleen asked.

"Well, I pray I am not being, too, forward. I would like to invite you to share a meal with me, if you will."

Kathleen stood dumbfounded, momentarily. "You are asking me out, Okency?"

"Yes, ma'am, I am. Nothing fancy, at first, unless you do not mind. I was thinking of the Olive Garden." Okency forged forward.

"Well, um…" Kathleen stammered. Her face felt flush. It had been t years since she had been asked on a date.

"Please say, 'yes,' Kathleen. It is just one meal. If you do not enjoy my company, I will not impose it upon you, ever again."

"Yes." Kathleen could not manage any other words. She was flabbergasted. Was this a test to see if she was walking out of the darkness of mourning?

"I am pleased. I will allow you a couple of days to process the request. If I may, I will excuse myself and anticipate our next meeting." Okency took her hand and kissed the back of it. He turned and walked into the corridor, leaving Kathleen standing alone in the auditorium.

~~~~~~~~~~~~~~~~~~~~~~~~~~

Kathleen pulled into the driveway of her home and turned off the radio. She was tempted to call Mother Salester, on her commute home, however she did not know what she wanted to say.

She locked the car door, after retrieving her briefcase from the backseat. Mother Salester opened the door as she was walking up the steps.

"How was your day, Kathleen?" Mother Salester asked, stepping aside to give Kathleen access to walk through the door.

"Mother, my day was interesting, to say the least." Kathleen stated, while closing the front door.

The two ladies walked into the kitchen and sat down at the table, as was their custom. Mother Salester had the teapot, cups and saucers waiting for her arrival. Kathleen loved having her mother-in-law in the house. She was great company and she was a tremendous spiritual comfort.

As she poured the tea, Mother Salester asked, "What made today more interesting than any other day?"

"Well, I was invited to the Olive Garden." Kathleen blushed.

"And...?" Mother Salester prompted.

"A gentleman, by the name of Okency McIntyre, asked me after my lecture. He is a professor of Military History, at the University." Kathleen added.

"I see. Did you answer him?"

"Yes, I did. I consented to one date."

"When will this date take place?" Mother Salester took a sip of tea

"Okency has allowed me a couple of days to let it all sink in."

"Okency McIntyre sounds very distinguished and quite the gentleman."

Kathleen took a few sips of her tea, before speaking. "He is polished. His features are well put together, if I may say so."

"You may say so."

"I happy for you, Kathleen. It will do you a world of good, to go out with this young man."

"A world of good, Mother Salester?" Kathleen asked.

"Yes. It is time you get out and let someone treat you like a lady. Someone to open the car door for you, pull out your chair at the table, and give you compliments. You deserve a chance to be happy with a man, again."

"Whoa, slow down, Mother Salester." Kathleen put her hand up. "I am not certain I am ready for all of that, just yet."

"You cannot sit around and wait to feel like dating or getting to know a man, again. It will be something you will have to test the waters with, so to speak." Mother Salester sipped.

"Are you speaking from experience or are you just passing out advice, arbitrarily?"

"I am not one to give arbitrary advice, sweetie. You know this about me, already. It was a few years after Joseph's father had passed. I was in a church meeting and one of the older deacons approached me. He said he wanted someone he could spend time with, so he asked me. I obliged." Mother Salester rose from the table, taking the dishes to the sink.

"I don't recall you going out with anyone, Mother Salester."

"There are still a few secrets, an old woman can keep." They laughed.

"What happened?" Kathleen asked.

"Well, we spent most of our time, together for a couple of years, then he took sick. He later died." A far-away looked appeared in Mother Salester's eyes.

"Did you love this man?"

"I loved him as much as I could, after losing the love of my life when Joseph's father died. I just couldn't bring myself to venture out, again." Mother Salester picked up the sponge and began to wash the dishes.

"I'm sorry." Kathleen consoled.

"Oh no, baby. Do not be sorry for me. I had a chance to love two good men. There are so many who cannot boast of one, let alone two." She dried her hands on the hand towel, which had been draped over the counter.

"I don't know if I am ready to take a chance on love, again. I'm afraid to lose anyone else. Joseph's death devastated me." Kathleen shook her head.

"God is able to keep your mind, if you keep your mind on Him. Yea, though you walk through the valley of the shadow of death, you shall fear no evil. Why?"

"Because the Lord is with me." Kathleen answered.

"That is right. God does not want us to walk around fearful of experiencing emotions. He wants us to trust that He will see us through to the other side, if the river gets a little high. You are a beautiful and desirable woman, Kathleen. Do not put yourself on the shelf, when you still have needs."

"Mother Salester!"

"I'm a woman, Kathleen. I may be old, but I am not dead. I know you still desire the company of a man. I do, sometimes."

"You do?"

"Don't look, so surprised! Yes, I do." Mother Salester laughed and swatted Kathleen's shoulder, playfully.

"I am not saying sleep with the man. I am saying enjoy the Olive Garden. See what he is like and if you want to get to know him better. There is nothing wrong with that." Mother Salester headed toward the living room.

"Now, you go take your bath and change your clothes. Dinner will be ready when you are finished. I have a roast, in the oven." Mother Salester sat down, on the sofa, and switched on the television.

"I will be down, in a short while." Kathleen headed toward the staircase, after picking up her briefcase, which had been placed on the bottom step when she came in the door.

CHAPTER THIRTY-ONE

Mother Salester awoke, with a start. She sensed, in her spirit, that a child was fighting for his/her life. She felt an urgent unction to intercede for this child. She arose from the bed and slid, slowly, down to her knees. Tears fell from her eyes as she felt God's compassion for this baby. The Holy Spirit spoke, quietly, to her spirit alerting her that an unborn child was in danger.

She reached for her bible, which she kept on the nightstand, beside the bed. She switched on the light and searched for Psalm one hundred thirty nine, after putting on her glasses. Mother Salester read aloud from verse thirteen through sixteen, *"For you created my inmost being; you knit me together in my mother's womb. I praise you because I am fearfully and wonderfully made; your works are wonderful, I know that full well. My frame was not hidden from you when I was made in the secret place. When I was woven together in the depths of the earth, your eyes saw my unformed body. All the days ordained for me were written in your book before one of them came to be."*

She placed the bible on the bed, as she bowed her head to pray. "Father, only You know what this child is going through. You know this precious little one, in a way no one else will. There are plans, in place, which You have orchestrated for her to fulfill. She belongs to You. Take care of her needs and stop the hand of the enemy from moving any further. The devil is looking to discourage and utterly tear down the parents of this little darling baby. You are our Encourager and the Lifter of our heads. Father, encourage the parents by blessing them with the life of this child that the doctors report will not live. Let her life be a testament to Your undying love and devotion to Your children. Overwhelm their hearts with the knowledge and acceptance of Your forgiveness, as this child was conceived outside of the boundary of a marriage covenant. Children are a gift and the father is blessed, whose quiver is full. Lord God, Great Jehovah Rapha – the Father of Abraham, Isaac and Jacob – our Father, through the covenant You wrought by the blood of Your dear Son, Jesus Christ. I thank You, right now, for the testimony that is being created, as I pray this prayer. I am rejoicing in the knowledge that You take pleasure in blessing and favoring Your people. We have been engrafted into the fold because of Your great love for mankind. In the book of Jeremiah You say, *for I know the plans I have for you, declares the Lord, plans to prosper you and not to harm you, plans to give you hope and a future.* I believe this to be so for the life of Your beloved angel; this child yet to take her first breath. She will live and not die to declare Your goodness, in the land of the living. This, I pray, decree and declare by the power You have given to me, through the name of Jesus Christ…Amen."

~~~~~~~~~~~~~~~~~~~~~~~~~~~~~~~

Ariel bolted upright in the bed and clutched her belly. She yelled out and reached over for Micah, as a pain gripped her that she had not experienced before. "Micah! Micah, wake up. Something is the matter!" There was a sense of urgency in her voice, as she noticed the sheets were soaked with her blood.

Micah turned on the lamp, beside the bed and gasped as Ariel pushed the covers back. "Oh my God, Ariel, you are bleeding!"

"Micah, I am frightened for the babies. They are not due for another two months." Ariel's eyes were wide, with fear.

"Okay. Okay." Micah attempted to assess the situation, without allowing his panic to become evident to his wife. "Where is the number to the doctor?"

"The number is on speed dial, just hit three, on the phone." Ariel cried.

Micah did as instructed, as he arose from the bed to get towels from the linen closet, in the bathroom. "Yes, hello. Is this Dr. Gatewood?"

Dr. Liam Gatewood was a tall man, some would call distinguished. His graying hair and weathered features made him the talk of the obstetrics department at Chesapeake Regional Medical Center. He was the doctor, on-call, when Micah dialed the emergency number for the practice.

"Yes, this is Dr. Gatewood. What is the emergency?" His deep baritone voice soothed Micah's nerves.

"This is Micah Alexander, you are the OB for my wife, Ariel Alexander."

"What is the emergency?" Dr. Gatewood repeated.

"Ariel is seven months pregnant, with twins. She is experiencing pain and she is bleeding." Micah tried to keep his voice as calm as the doctor's.

"I am familiar with her situation. I would suggest you bring her in, immediately. I will inform the nurses, at the desk, and they will have a room prepared for her when you arrive. I will, also, alert Dr. Heather Manson. She is the pediatric oncologist that has been on consult in your wife's care." Dr. Gatewood's voice never sounded alarmed or harried, as he spoke to Micah. "Do you think you can assess how much blood has been lost? If you press on the mattress is there a sufficient amount of blood that it pools around your finger?"

Micah leaned over and pressed the blood stain, on the bed. There was a small amount of pooling. "There is a small amount of pooling, however, I cannot determine if the mattress is absorbing any of the blood."

"Fair enough. Let's get off of the line, so you can get here, quickly. I will be waiting."

The line went dead and Micah replaced the receiver onto the cradle. "Baby, we need to get you up, so we can get to the hospital. The doctors will be waiting." He rounded the bed to help Ariel get up. Her night clothes were soaked with blood and Micah felt panic rise up into his throat. *Now was not the time to get queasy and faint of heart*, he said to himself.

Ariel imagined she was dreaming, as she allowed Micah to remove her clothing, and help her into the shower. He rinsed her down, toweled her dry and dressed her. She could hear him speaking to her, as if he were in a fog.

"Help me, baby."

She lifted her leg, at the appropriate time for panties and pants. She raised her arms for her bra and shirt. Micah brushed her hair, while she sat on the side of the bed. Micah rushed to get himself dressed, packed a bag for Ariel, and then led her gently to the car.

When they arrived at the hospital, Micah jumped out of the car in search of a wheelchair. Once located, he wheeled it to the passenger side of his car. He opened the car door and carefully assisted his dazed wife into the seat. He, quickly, made his way to the bay of elevators and pushed the button.

The doctors and nurses were at the desk, awaiting their arrival, as promised.

"I will take her from here, Mr. Alexander." One of the nurse's spoke.

"Where will you be taking her?" Micah questioned.

Another nurse was at his side. "Your wife is in good hands, Mr. Alexander. She will be in room two twenty two, where they will hook her up to a monitor to assess the condition of the twins. Dr. Gatewood will, also, examine her to determine where the origin of the bleeding." Her voice was soft and calm.

"Will I be able to be with her?" Micah asked.

"Of course, you will. We will help her out of her clothes and into a hospital gown, while you park your car."

"Oh yes, the car." In the hustle and bustle he had left the keys in the ignition and the doors open. "I hope there is still a car there." Micah laughed nervously.

"The security guard has been keeping an eye on the vehicle. He called up, as soon as he determined the situation."

"Thank you."

Before the nurse could utter a word, a loud alarm sounded behind the desk. She ran to determine which room needed help. The nurse looked, worriedly, at Micah. "Hurry, Mr. Alexander. They are prepping your wife for an emergency Caesarian section. If you don't mind, I will ask security to park your car, then bring your keys to the nurses desk."

Micah nodded his consent. While rushing down the hall, the nurse stepped out of Ariel's room. "We need a crash cart, stat. The patient is coding."

CHAPTER THIRTY-TWO

The ringing of the telephone startled Damaris out of a deep sleep. She switched on the bedside lamp, wondering who could be calling at this hour. She looked at the caller ID and was surprised to see it was Preston.

"Hey there, sweetie." Damaris answered, groggily.

"Hey, baby." Preston replied. "I just received an urgent call from Micah. He had to rush her to the hospital. She awakened in pain and there was some bleeding, from what I could gather."

Damaris jumped from the bed and ran to her closet to pull out something to throw on. "Oh my goodness, Preston...is everything, alright?"

"The last thing I heard him say, was they were getting ready to rush her into the operating room for emergency surgery, before her heart stopped." Preston was already dressed and headed for the garage.

"WHAT?" Damaris screamed, into the phone.

"I am getting into my car, right now, headed over to your place. I do not want you to have to drive. Micah asked if you could tell the girls." Preston turned the key in the ignition and the engine revved.

Damaris burst into tears and fell to the floor. "Oh God, please keep my friend safe and her babies, as well."

"Are you going to be okay until I get there, Damaris?" Preston was backing the car out of the garage and onto the street.

"I will call MJ and Sela. I am sure they will meet us at the hospital. I will be waiting for you. Preston, please hurry."

As soon as Preston got off the line, Damaris was dialing Garrison and MJ's house. A sleepy MJ answered the phone.

"Hey girl, this better be an emergency." MJ stated.

"It's Ariel. She is in trouble and she needs us. Preston called after talking with a frantic Micah stating her heart had stopped after she began bleeding." Damaris was trying to speak, calmly.

"Are you kidding me? What kind of craziness is this?" MJ shouted.

Damaris could hear Garrison in the background, and then muffled talking as MJ apprised him of the situation.

"I am going to call Sela, so the two of you can get ready and meet us at Chesapeake Regional Medical Center." Damaris hung up, and then quickly dialed Sela's number.

"Who the hell is this calling my house at this ungodly hour?" Sela yelled into the phone.

"Sela, this is Damaris. Ariel has been rushed to Chesapeake Regional. She is bleeding and is gravely sick." Damaris hurried.

"What in the world? What happened?" Sela hopped from the bed and ran to her bathroom, to splash some water on her face.

"I do not have all of the particulars, just that Micah told Preston there was some bleeding, then her heart stopped while they were preparing her for emergency surgery." Damaris rambled off the details as she was given them.

"Let me get myself together, and I will be right up there." Sela hung up, quickly.

Preston honked the horn and Damaris grabbed her bag and ran out of the door. She hopped in the passenger seat, just before Preston sped out of her driveway. She held his hand and they prayed, as he sped toward the hospital.

"Lord, this is not unto death." They professed, as Preston searched for a parking space, just outside of the emergency room entrance. He noticed Micah's truck, in a spot near the door and he pulled his car, next to it.

Preston jumped out of the car and grabbed Damaris' hand as she was closing the passenger side door. They rushed through the doors and up to the maternity ward.

"We are here to get some information on our friend, Ariel Alexander." Preston addressed the nurse behind the desk.

"All I can tell you is that she is in surgery." The nurse explained.

"Thank God, she is alive." Damaris sighed.

"Yes, she is." The nurse assured her. "You can have a seat, in the waiting area. As soon as there is news, I will have Mr. Alexander or the doctor come in to speak with you."

"Thank you, very much." Preston addressed the nurse. "There will be others, who will be up here, please direct them to us. We will let them know what is going on."

"I surely will."

Damaris and Preston headed in the direction of the waiting room and took their seats. Tears were falling down her cheeks, freely.

"Everything will be alright, Damaris. God does not fail. We have to trust Him." Preston comforted.

"I know. It is just so much, on her." Damaris cried.

"No more than the Father knows she can bear. It may seem like an insurmountable obstacle, at the moment. Isaiah forty-two, verse three, assures us that a bruised reed He will not break. He will not overburden her, causing her break. He is at work, on her behalf, right now." Preston took Damaris into his arms.

"I know, you are right, Preston." Damaris calmed.

"We serve a just and fair God. He heals, delivers and sets us free. He does all things, completely and wonderfully. Ariel and the babies will all be just fine, once it is all said and done." Preston assured.

"Thank you. I am grateful for your presence, in my life. God knew I would need you." Damaris kissed Preston's cheek, gently.

"Yes, He did. Now dry those beautiful eyes of yours and begin to rejoice, in your spirit. A miracle is taking place." Preston's smile showed forth his confidence.

Damaris smiled, too. She was confident that God was doing a good work, using the hands of the surgeons. As she wiped her eyes, Sela, Garrison and MJ walked into the waiting room.

The five friends waited, together. There was little conversation being made. Garrison held MJ in his arms, while Damaris held Sela's hand; Preston put his arm around her shoulder.

After a couple of hours, a bedraggled Micah walked into the waiting room.

"The surgery is over." Micah burst into tears, as Preston and Garrison hurried to his side, before he collapsed onto the floor.

CHAPTER THIRTY-THREE

The dawn sky seemed bleak and dreary. Dark clouds blanketed the city, gearing it up for another rainy day. Aaron hopped out of bed, heading for the thermostat. There was a chill, in the house, and he did not want Tamu to wake up and be cold.

Aaron hurried back to bed and snuggled close to Tamu. She stirred and nestled her behind into his pelvis. "Bonjour, le bien-aimé." She whispered.

"Good morning, to you. I love it when you speak French to me, in that sexy voice of yours." Aaron put his arm around Tamu's waist.

"I know it. Vous faire a quelque chose pour moi?" Tamu asked.

Aaron kissed her neck, softly. "Oh yes, I do have something for you, baby girl."

Tamu giggled, recognizing his gift. "Me le donner, le papa." She arched her back and reached her hand back to grab Aaron's head. She turned to meet his emblazoned kiss.

"Daddy is going to give it to you." He lifted Tamu, so her body was lying atop of his and he grabbed her hips.

"Je veux tout." Tamu gasped, as Aaron complied.

~~~~~~~~~~~~~~~~~~~~~

Tamu walked into the Dominion Counseling and Wellness Center, with a smile on her face. She loved waking up with Aaron on rainy days. He seemed to be in rare form with the skies open up. A pang ran through her belly as she thought of the things he did to her, this morning.

She walked into her office and clicked on the answering machine, as was her custom. With pencil, in hand, she commenced to writing down important names and numbers that she would have to get back to, this morning. Tamu dropped the pencil when she listened to Mary's message.

"Tamu, I apologize. I will not be able to make it into work, today. A dear friend of mine had a major medical emergency over the weekend and I am drained. I wish I could say she is out of the woods, but I cannot. I feel it is my obligation to be there, in case matters change." Mary's voice sounded weary and Tamu could hear the evidence of recent crying.

Tamu knew that Mary was close with Damaris, the woman Preston is dating. She hoped the emergency did not have anything to do with her. She said a silent prayer for whoever the woman was, and then proceeded to listen to the remainder of the messages.

Her office phone rang, just as she clicked on the answering machine. "Dominion Counseling and Wellness Center, Tamu Singletary speaking, how can I help you?" She answered.

"I want to tell you that your form of medicine is the panacea for all that ails me." Aaron was speaking. "I need another dose, Doctor."

Tamu blushed, as she felt a familiar ache in the pit of her stomach. "Aaron, you need to stop it. You are causing me to ache"

"I can be there in twenty minutes for an office visit." Aaron offered.

"Je vous attendrai." Tamu accepted.

"You will not have to wait long. I will soothe that ache for you, baby girl." Aaron replied.

Tamu felt flush with excitement. There is nothing like seconds when the food is good, she thought to herself. She walked toward the wall of windows that looked out into the entrance, and pulled the blinds. She did not want to think of anything, once Aaron arrived, except what he was going to do to her. She shivered just thinking about it.

Aaron hung up the phone, smiling. He loved his life. He was the Regional Director of Finance at one of the largest investment companies in the state. He made the money he wanted to make and he had the freedom to come and go, as he pleased. His secretary has the number to his Blackberry, if an urgent matter arise which needs his direct attention. He traveled around the country, on business trips, which allowed him experiences he may not have had, otherwise.

Then there was Tamu. She was five years his senior, but she kept in time with whatever he wanted. She cleared her calendar every time he requested her company on his trips. He knew that freedom came along with her being the owner of her business. She was successful, accomplished, beautiful and sexy. She was devoted to him and their relationship. He could not ask for a better woman.

There were younger women who approached him, looking for a good time. He didn't pay them any attention. He knew what he had, at home, and he was not going to mess up his good thing. Besides, he thought, those women weren't about anything. They were looking for a guy to take care of them, so they can sit back and do nothing. Aaron did not understand why women thought that was attractive. It was unproductive, trifling as his grandmother would say. No man who is looking to achieve great things would be satisfied with a woman whose only goal is to be a trophy piece.

Aaron was not dull-witted. He knew there were ball players, drug dealers and rap artists who may be looking for a woman of that caliber. He was not that man, nor was any of the men he associated with, in his circle.

As he pulled into the parking lot of the Dominion Counseling and Wellness Center, he smiled. He is proud to call Tamu Singletary his woman. Mother Salester told him he should marry her, before she tires of waiting. He sighed. He knew he didn't want to live his life without her. He felt like marriage would change what they had. He knew his mother and father had a loving and long-lasting relationship, but he thought it was due to their generation.

Nowadays, people just didn't hold fast to the same values his parents had. As it stands, both he and Tamu were satisfied with the status quo. She never nagged him or whined about getting married. She didn't complain about being taken advantage of or not feeling appreciated, in their relationship. Why mess with a good thing?

He parked his Lincoln Navigator, in a parking spot away from the building. He did not want to occupy space that her clients were going to need. He hopped down from the truck, adjusted his clothes, pushed the remote control and locked the doors.

He walked quickly to the entryway and headed toward Tamu's office. His excitement was becoming evident, as he opened the door. Tamu stood by her desk in her stockings, garter belt, bra and panties. He clicked the lock on the door, with one hand, as he began to unbuckle his belt with the other.

CHAPTER THIRTY-FOUR

Weeks passed, without much change to Ariel's condition. She lived through the Caesarean section and the subsequent hysterectomy. However, she lost so much blood that her organs failed and sent her into cardiac arrest. Now, she lay in a coma, after suffering a stroke, in the intensive care unit of Chesapeake Regional Memorial Hospital.

The placenta which had been nourishing Nasarra broke away from Ariel's uterine wall causing a massive hemorrhage. The doctors were able to able to deliver the babies, which were now in the neonatal intensive care unit. Nasir was delivered weighing just over three pounds, while his sister, Nasarra weighed in a little over two and a half pounds. After undergoing a battery of exams, by Dr. Manson's team of pediatric oncologists, the brain mass had mysteriously disappeared.

Damaris and Preston clapped their hands and shouted for joy, at the news. God had performed a miracle for their goddaughter and they praised Him for it, heartily. They were a constant presence at the hospital, giving Micah an opportunity to go home and get some rest. They kept vigil at Ariel's bedside and with the twins, as often as they were allowed. They had been given clearance for the doctors and nurses to report to them in the instance Micah was not present.

The three comrades sat in the hospital's cafeteria talking about the strides the twins had made in their weight gain and lung maturity. Nasir had gained a full pound and half and his sister packed on an impressive two pounds. They were breathing on their own, and would soon be allowed to leave the neonatal intensive care unit.

"The babies are beautiful, Micah." Damaris said.

"They really are." Preston agreed.

"I will be glad when their mother can look at them and hold them." Micah added.

"Soon enough, man. Soon enough." Preston encouraged.

"I am excited to hear news of the stem cell transplant, with Ariel. I know it was a risky decision to attempt the transplant without the backing of the entire medical community, but the doctors were hopeful, even with the controversy surrounding the procedure." Damaris took a bite of her tuna sandwich.

"I am grateful Ariel did not listen to me and had a written order for the doctor to collect the cord blood from the babies." Micah shook his head.

"Don't be down on yourself. It is in the past. Let it be." Preston stated.

Damaris had been researching cord blood and its many uses, once Sela had brought up the topic, with Ariel. Stem cell transplants are being touted as a revolutionary treatment for many acute and chronic forms of leukemia, as well as other malignancies. They can be harvested from umbilical cord blood, as well as embryos and some adult tissue.

Stem cells have the ability to renew themselves through mitotic cell division and differentiating into a diverse range of specialized cell types. There was much debate, on the topic, as early researchers believed embryonic stem cells should be used. Pro-life campaigners were against this research as it cost the embryo its life. Recent studies have found they can get the same benefit from using the cord blood.

Damaris read that researchers hold out the hope that stem cells can be coaxed into becoming any other type of cell in the body, holding out the possibility of growing replacement tissue or even organs.

"The blood taken from the babies' umbilical cords was an excellent source of stem cells needed to treat Ariel's stroke." Damaris informed.

"Like I said, I am glad she didn't listen to me." Micah insisted.

They finished their lunch and headed back to sit with Ariel. As they filed out of the elevator, the nurse informed that Ariel's doctor would like to speak with Micah. He headed to the office, while Damaris and Preston walked toward the waiting room.

"Excuse me." The nurse interrupted the couple.

"Yes?" Damaris answered.

"I have been informed that the twins have been taken off of the ventilator and they are breathing on their own." The nurse informed.

"That is splendid news!" Preston exclaimed.

"Praise the Lord." Damaris added.

They continued into the waiting room, praying that the news from Ariel's doctor was equally as wonderful.

~~~~~~~~~~~~~~~~~~~~~~~

When Micah left the doctor's office, he was on cloud nine. He had been given the good news that the recent MRI showed that cells had migrated to damaged area of Ariel's brain. There has been a significant improvement in her brain's function and she showed signs of reversal.

The doctor advised this was a case study for the medical journals, as research was still underway for the use of stem cells for stroke victims. This was an unprecedented flip of the coin, as the doctor described it, and it seems like they won the toss.

Micah hurried to tell Preston and Damaris the good news. As he opened the door, of the waiting room, he was assailed with their exciting news about the babies.

"God is so good." Micah shouted. "The doctor just told me that the experimental stem cell transplant seems to be doing the trick. The latest MRI shows a near complete reversal of the damaged area of her brain."

Immediately Damaris began to cry, as Preston shouted a hearty 'hallelujah' into the air. "We serve a mighty God!" He continued.

"Yes, we do!" Micah agreed, as tears ran down his cheeks. "God has saved my family." He began to weep, aloud. He fell to his knees and began to repent for everything. He cried out to God as he recommitted himself to the Lord and his wife. He was unashamed, as he cleared his plate with his heavenly Father. He didn't want anything between him and his relationship with God and his family.

Preston and Damaris stood by, reverent of the moment; each taking inventory of their own lives and laying them out before God, silently. They held each other's hand and prayed for one another, along with Micah and his family.

When Micah stood, they embraced for a long moment, before heading out to visit with Nasir and Nasarra Alexander.

CHAPTER THIRTY-FIVE

PRESTON WAS LEFT BREATHLESS, as he watched Damaris walk down the aisle. He had thought of this moment, for months, and still could not have imagined a more beautiful sight.

Damaris smiled, as she witnessed the reaction on his face. Tears welled up, as she anticipated being held in his arms. She missed him. The last time she had laid eyes on Preston, was a week ago. It was a mutual agreement to allow themselves the time to commune with God, prior to their union. Now, as she caressed his face with her eyes, she was more in love than ever. She felt as if she was walking on clouds, as she moved closer and closer to the man God had chosen for her.

Preston was corralled by an intense restraint, as he stood in place waiting for his bride. A grin seemed to stretch his face, beyond its limit. He felt like he was beaming with pride. He silently thanked God, as he had done countless times before, for leading him to his destiny. Damaris Rhenay was his wife. He knew it, just as he knew his name was Preston Lambert.

They had waited for this day, for months. After Ariel's miraculous recovery from the hemorrhage and subsequent stroke after having the babies, Preston and Damaris wanted to get married, at the earliest date. The situation that occurred with their friends, every moment mattered. The two of them did not want to waste any time they could be sharing their lives, together, as husband and wife.

Ariel went through physical and occupational therapy which assisted her to get back on her feet so she could take care of the twins. Damaris was by her side, coaxing and encouraging her friend whenever depression loomed over her head. The road was long, however God saw fit to see them through it.

Damaris smiled, deeply, as she looked over to her bridesmaid to see Ariel standing amongst her friends. What an awesome God, Damaris thought. He has seen them all through some intense battles.

Now, as her father released her into the care of her soon-to-be husband, tears fell down her cheeks. She watched, as her dad took his seat next to her mother and noticed tears on their faces.

"You look exquisite." Preston whispered in her ear.

Damaris felt like a princess in the Sue Wong original; a dramatic skirt of pure white ostrich feathers, sequins dotted the entire dress – giving her just the right sparkle, as she waltzed down the aisle. The tulle under the hem of the dress gave if fullness, at the bottom, and the fitted drop waist bodice tantalized Preston as he looked down at his bride, standing at his side.

The couple wrote their own vows. After the necessary verbiage, from the pastor, they were able to speak their hearts.

"I, Preston Lambert, take you, Damaris Rhenay, to be my wife, my partner in life; you are my one true love. I cherish our friendship. I love you today; I will love you tomorrow, and forever. I trust you and honor you and will do so for the rest of my life; I will laugh with you and cry with you. I will love you faithfully, through the best and the worst, through the difficult and the easy. What may come I will always be there. I have given you my heart and I give you my life to keep, as I invite you to share my life. I promise always to respect your needs. I will endeavor through kindness, unselfishness and trust to achieve the warm rich life we now look forward to."

"I, Damaris Rhenay, take you, Preston Lambert, to be husband, my partner in life; my one true love. I, too, cherish our friendship and the kindred spirits we possess. From this day forward I promise that I will laugh with you in times of joy and comfort you in times of sorrow. I will share in your dreams, and support you as you strive to achieve your goals. I will listen to you with compassion and understanding, and speak to you with encouragement. I will help you when you need it, and step aside when you don't. I will remain faithful to you for better or worse, in times of sickness and health. I will love and respect you always."

The pastor asked for the rings and he held them in his hands, as he prayed. "Father, I hold in my hands the symbol of the covenant that Preston and Damaris has pledged in their hearts. It is an unending circle of life, perpetually flowing from one end to the other. This is what you desire for them, as husband and wife, that their lives be forever encircled around one another. Your will is for them to be one, causing them to be inseparable in the spirit of unity. Lord, they may not always agree, in their discourse, they will always agree in You.

Bind them together, in Your love and teach them to love one another, perfectly. Consecrate and sanctify them and these rings, in the name of Jesus, I pray...Amen."

After repeating the customary lines in the exchange of the rings, the pastor confirmed, "By the power vested in me, by God and this Commonwealth of Virginia, I now pronounce you husband and wife. Preston, you may salute your bride."

Preston pulled the veil back, as he drew his wife close. Damaris reached up, wrapping her arms around his neck and kissed him, passionately. The pastor cleared his throat and the congregation laughed.

"There will be plenty of time for that." He joked. "Now, will you all rise. I present to you, for the very first time, Mr. and Mrs. Preston and Damaris Lambert."

The congregation cheered and applauded, as the couple walked down from the pulpit, hand in hand. The bridal party followed behind them to form the reception line, just outside of the church.

~~~~~~~~~~~~~~~~~~~~~~~~~

Preston and Damaris hopped in the Lincoln Limousine they had reserved as their private transportation to the wedding reception. The driver had been alerted, earlier to have the privacy partition, in place prior to his arrival. There was champagne chilling in the cooler and mood lighting had been turned on, as they took their seats.

Damaris leaned close to Preston and licked his lips, softly with her tongue, as he opened his mouth. She leaned her head back, as he kissed her chin, her neck and the lobes of her ears. A soft moan, escaped her as the trail of kisses led to the exposed portions of her breasts.

"I love this dress and the way it accents what looks to be beautiful breasts." Preston stated.

"Take a look at them, they are all yours, now." Damaris offered.

Preston reached behind his wife and loosed the hook and eye enclosure, then unzipped the zipper. Damaris' breasts were exposed and he smiled.

"Just like I imagined." He kissed each one, slowly.

Damaris loosed Preston's tie and unbuttoned his shirt, reaching her hands inside to caress his chest. She pressed her breasts close to his chest, as she kissed him deeply.

"I have a surprise for you." Damaris whispered in his ear.

"Surprise me, baby."

She took Preston's hands, slid them slowly up her thighs and under her dress. Damaris was kissing the spot on his neck just behind his ear. She moved them, steadily upward, until he could feel his long awaited treasure.

"Oh, baby." Preston sighed.

"Yes, just for you." Damaris breathed.

"Thank you." Preston laid Damaris back on the car seat, while pushing up the feathered skirt and tulle. He unsnapped the garter belt and rolled down her stockings, following the nylons with kisses.

A gasp escaped her lips as Preston's mouth met her surprise with ardent fervor. His kisses were deep and lingering. Damaris could not remember a feeling quite as tantalizing as his tongue and mouth on her body.

She pulled Preston up to kiss her. Damaris felt sensual and sexy, as she removed the evidence from his lips. He lifted her from the seat and onto his lap. She hadn't realized when he had loosened his belt or lowered his pants.

Damaris could not take deep breaths as Preston entered her. A host of small fires were set in her belly and her body was aflame. Goose bumps rose over her arms and legs, as he gently rocked with her until they were spent.

She collapsed onto his shoulder and wept. Preston kissed the tears as the fell onto her cheeks.

"I am in love with an incredible woman." He spoke, softly.

"And I, with an incredible man." She replied.

~~~~~~~~~~~~~~~~~~~~~~~~

The limousine pulled up to the door of the Grand Affairs, in Virginia Beach. The driver knocked on the privacy partition to insure the occupants were ready to depart from the vehicle. Preston pushed the intercom button.

"Yes?" Preston called out.

"We have arrived at the destination, sir. Are you and your bride ready to depart?" The driver questioned.

"Yes, we are. Thank you for the consideration." Preston held back a laugh.

"You are welcome. I will be around to open the door for the two of you."

"I appreciate it."

Damaris fixed Preston's tie, after she replaced her stockings; fastening them to the garter belt. He had taken great care not to mess up her hair, so the only thing to straighten out was her dress.

The driver opened the door, allowing the bride and groom to step out of the vehicle onto the carpeted walkway. Preston and Damaris were escorted to the doorway of one of their many ballrooms, by their wedding planner. She motioned toward the deejay, alerting him to put on their wedding song.

"Ladies and gentlemen, I present to you the guests of honor, Mr. and Mrs. Preston Lambert." The deejay announced, prior to letting the record play.

Preston took Damaris' hand and walked her to the middle of the ballroom floor. The words from BeBe/CeCe Winans, I Found Love filled the room. He twirled her around, before pulling her close. He whispered the lyrics as they glided in perfect synergy.

"When I found you, I found someone who cares. When I found you, found my most intimate prayer. When I found you, I found what every heart dreams of; when I found you, I found love."

Damaris picked up the song, "When I found you, I found my fate in your arms. When I found you, I found no cause for alarm. When I found you, I knew this love was a gift from above. When I found you, I found love."

They kissed and danced until the song ended and their guests applauded. They walked over to the table for the bridal party and took their seats.

There was an array of dishes on their table; cold canapés, shrimp shooters, along with fruit & cheese with a flowing chocolate fountain, in the center.

After the appetizers were removed from the table the wait staff presented the guests with a seasonal salad with an assortment of dressings from which to choose. They served country green beans, Lynnhaven crab cakes with sauce remoulade, Williamsburg orange-pecan glazed chicken, new potatoes and dinner rolls, with iced tea.

There was a dessert table, to the left of the wedding cake, which was five tiers of strawberry shortcake (the couple's favorite). Preston led Damaris to the table in order to cut the cake.

Preston scooped some of the cake onto his fingers, and slowly put it into Damaris' mouth. She closed her lips around his fingers and swirled her tongue across each one, then kissed his fingertips.

"Wait a minute!" Sela called from the crowd. "Church people do this kind of stuff?"

Everyone laughed and the music began to play. Couples moved to the middle of the floor to dance and have a good time. Damaris and Preston returned to their seats. Sela and Jeremiah were at the table, as well.

Sela leaned in to speak to the couple. "I know what you two did. Ooohh, ya'll are little freaks."

Damaris blushed. "Sela!"

"Don't 'Sela' me, little Miss Hot Mama." Sela replied.

"You are embarrassing me." Damaris whispered.

"Why you embarrassed? He is your husband, no shame from the old biddies at the church. They know they get down with the get down, too." Sela continued, "Was it good, girl?"

"I can't even think about it, without getting chills."

"He laid it on you, huh?" Sela leaned passed Damaris and spoke to Preston. "Do it, Papa!"

"Sela!" Damaris insisted.

"I'm happy for you, girl. I'm real happy for you." Sela sat back in her chair, whispering to Jeremiah.

Preston shook his head, laughing, as he caressed Damaris' leg, under the table. He leaned in, kissing her lips. "I can't wait to get you to the hotel room."

Damaris gasped, as Preston's hand hinted toward the evening's festivities. "Me either." She sighed.

EPILOGUE

Mother Salester sat in the front seat of the First Lady's car, as she escorted a group of the seniors to an evangelistic outreach they had planned.

The Silver Years was a group of the elder patrons of the church which got together a couple of times during the month. They talked about their families, their changing needs as older members of society and planned outings to keep themselves busy.

This particular Saturday afternoon was one such event. The group used their funds to purchase bibles and tracts and they were going out into the community to talk about the good news of Jesus. The First Lady offered to chauffer them, remaining in the area, in case one of the members needed a break from walking.

The group was well received as they handed bibles to the children and teens. They went from house to house to pass out tracts and see if there was a need for prayer.

Mother Salester and Sister Hattie walked toward one home, as the others were ministering to a group of young people, on the corner. They rang the bell and chatted with each other, as they waited.

"Who is that ringing my god..." The door flung open and a young man appeared.

"Good afternoon, young man." Mother Salester greeted, reaching out her hand to shake his.

"What do you want, old lady." The young man insisted.

"I just want to share the good news of the Lord, with you, today."

"Good news, huh?" He questioned.

"Yes." Hattie picked up. "God loves you, and His Son died to save you from hell."

Mother Salester felt the quickening of the Holy Spirit, as she saw the shadow of a man walk across behind the young man at the door.

"We are not here to harm or disgruntle you." She spoke to the figure in the background. "We want you to know that no matter your past, God loves you."

As the words were leaving her mouth, she heard the sound of a rifle being cocked.

Mother Salester quietly prayed, "Father forgive him."

She felt a searing pain in her chest and the warmth of her blood spread down her torso. "Tell God, I don't want his love." Were the last words she heard before her spirit left her body.

There were screams in the street and from Hattie, as they realized what had taken place.

"You want some, too, old lady. If not, you better take your God and get to steppin'." The shadow shouted from behind the young man in the doorway.

Hattie hurried off of the porch, toward the other members of the group. First Lady dialed 9-1-1 on her cell phone, as she pulled up to the corner and urged them to get into the car.

Keyvaughn Wells steps out onto the porch, picked up Mother Salester's lifeless body and carried her to the sidewalk and drops her. "Don't forget her." He yelled toward the car.